Brainstorm

A Novel

Joe Kremer

 OLD STONE PRESS

Brainstorm
By Joe Kremer

Published by Old Stone Press
an imprint of J. H. Clark & Associates, Inc.
Louisville, Kentucky 40207 USA
www.oldstonepress.com

© 2020, Joe Kremer

All rights reserved.

For information about special discounts for bulk purchases or autographed
copies of this book, please contact John H. Clark, publisher, Old Stone
Press at john@oldstonepress.com or the author, Joe Kremer at
joe_kremer_99@yahoo.com.

Library of Congress Control Number: 2020913366

ISBN: 978-1-938462-45-0 (print)
ISBN: 978-1-938462-46-7 (eBook)

Published in the United States

Thanks to Kathy Kremer, the love of my life and the best person I know. Kathy bravely tramped through the high weeds that were the early first drafts of this book and could be relied on to tell me the truth and not just what I wanted to hear.

Author's Note

One hundred thousand people in this country will receive shock treatments for severe depression this year. No one knows why electroconvulsive therapy works or what happens when a hundred watts of electricity is fired into the brain. But this is the story of what happened to me.

CHAPTER ONE

It was just the kind of spring day the planners of the first Kentucky Derby had in mind when they picked that time of year for their grand horse race. There had been early morning rain and then the sun broke through. Now the city glistened like a picture postcard. Pink and white blossoms were bursting on dogwoods, and the slender tendrils of weeping cherry trees draped like ribbons on a present. Against a background of lush bluegrass lawns, tulips of red, white and yellow struck poses along sidewalks and in gardens.

On my morning run through Seneca Park, the air I sucked into my lungs was sharply crisp and clean. In the home stretch, I sprinted past a relief cut in the pavement that served as my own personal finish line, hit the "Stop" button on my watch and saw I had a new course record. Hands on my knees to catch my breath, I looked up to see my wife, Gwen, leaning into the railing at the corner of our deck. Her eyes were closed, her head tilted up to allow the sun to paint a bit of color on her winter pale. She turned toward me and short blond hair glowed from the sun creating a golden frame around her face. She stood like a figurehead goddess on the prow of a ship. As soon as I could catch my breath, I would say, "God, you're beautiful." Before I could, Gwen looked down at me, smiled and said, "Paxton, I want a divorce."

Out of breath and sucker punched, I recognized the finality of the statement from the familiar tone in her voice. A discussion was not to be, this door had been slammed in my face. Beads of sweat rolled down my forehead and merged with the sudden flood in my eyes.

"I've taken a transfer to Jacksonville. I leave on Monday," she said as she turned and went back into the apartment. Jacksonville. Gwen worked in accounting at ADT Security. She would frequently mention her boss and sometimes in a dreamy kind of, "Brent did..." or "Brent said..." The last time his name was mentioned it was, "Brent was promoted to run the Jacksonville office." The picture came into focus.

Gwen hadn't said no to my proposal of marriage nine years before, but she thought we should get an apartment and try living together first. I was just happy to get her into my bed on a permanent basis, so that worked for me. I gave up the modern apartment complex where I lived with a heated pool, a gym and lots of other twenty-something singles, and Gwen flew away from the home nest. We merged our incomes, and I was happy to trade a pool for a garage that would save me from scraping frost off the car windows in the winter.

About a year into this new arrangement, we were out for a jog in the park. Gwen, who had run high school track, had a fifty-yard lead when she detoured off the paved path onto a cross-country trail. I spotted the mischievous smile on her face as she peeked over her shoulder to see if I would follow. I did. I weaved my way through thick brush and found her leaning languidly against a tree, a thumb tugging at the waist band of her shorts. From the index finger of her other hand her sports bra swung back and forth. The unplanned pregnancy that followed prompted us to reconsider marriage. Gwen had insisted we keep the pregnancy secret from her parents because she wanted to tell them "at the right time." It turned out the right time would be after her well-to-do parents had doled out the dough for the big wedding of her dreams. Gwen's mother did something important with the board of education and her father day-traded stocks from a home office. Money was not a problem.

I don't have any sisters, but I had been taught by TV sit-coms that girls had dreams of their perfect wedding at a very young age. So instead of thinking Gwen was being scheming and manipulative in not telling her parents she was pregnant, I chose to think she was cute.

Marriage plans were under way and Gwen had a playbook. She guided me along the way. One day after work, I turned on our shared computer and found a photo of a ring with a big round diamond surrounded by tiny emeralds set in platinum. This is the kind of hint I can track. The diamond shrank considerably and the mounting was changed to white gold to save money but Gwen was happy anyway.

Twelve weeks into the pregnancy and a month before the wedding, Gwen miscarried.

CHAPTER TWO

I spent the next few days doing two things at once. I followed her around as she packed begging for her to give "us" another chance and I began consuming large quantities of alcohol. Both efforts were counter-productive. Gwen went about her business, ignoring me, with nothing to say. As always, she was organized, consulting a list on her phone she had made up well before she dropped the divorce bomb on me. Her ducks stood at attention in neat rows. Three horrible days, two cases of beer, and she was gone.

When some of her work friends showed up at 7AM Monday to load Gwen's U-Haul, I was already a little swizzled. "Anybody wanna beer," I shouted as I opened my second. "It's not just for breakfast anymore."

Before she drove off, Gwen handed me her attorney's business card and said, "Sorry Pax."

I am an EMT for the city. To be precise, I'm an A-EMT: Advanced Emergency Medical Technician. My degree is in social work but that wasn't a good fit and I gave it up after five years. As a social worker in a nursing home, I didn't feel like I was doing much good. I had compassion for the residents in the home, I could help make them comfortable, provide entertainment and health care, but I was never going to be able to help them overcome their biggest obstacle, their age.

Private ambulances made daily runs to the nursing home. They sometimes delivered new residents, and often took old residents to the hospital or funeral home. Our ambulance bay was designed to be out of sight from visitors and patients in the back of the building and that is where I first met EMTs. I talked to them about what their typical day was like. Compared to my job, this EMT stuff was exciting. I learned that, unlike the private ambulance companies I saw every day, the med techs for Louisville's EMS didn't do transfers like I saw at the nursing home. Working for the city's emergency medical service was a wild ride of excitement. Hurtling through the streets, flashing lights and screaming siren, people rushing to get out of the way, the heroes on their way to save lives and do good. Sign me up.

But the downside of the job was getting to me these days. We're on the scene of every horrible tragedy that happens in this city. The frustration of getting to an accident too late or seeing the situation is hopeless is depressing. This downside goes a long way in explaining a burnout rate of twelve months, with divorce, alcoholism, and suicide rates that are right up there at the top of the charts with police and firefighters.

I called in sick for a week after Gwen left in order to examine my problems methodically. I was conducting a medical experiment to see if there was one brand of beer that was better at solving all my problems than any other. My experiment was thorough, scientific, and sure to pass any peer review. The winning brew was the cheapest swill Walmart had on the shelf when I stumbled in.

I had been experimenting a lot since the day Gwen drove out of my life, but I sobered up enough a week later to make my shift on time. My partner that week was Angela Barton. I didn't have to answer her question of, "How was your weekend?" because she read the answer in my face as soon as she asked. Angela extended a flat palm in a fierce imitation of a school crossing guard. "I'll drive," she said. We did a quick inventory and restock of our unit and were on the road fifteen minutes later.

Angela Barton is an Army trained paramedic with two tours in Afghanistan on her resume. She wants to be the first medic at every scene because she knows there is no paramedic who will do a better job. When we deliver a patient to the ER, Angela talks and the docs listen. It is respect she has earned.

Louisville EMS has 128 EMTs, which leaves us sixty people short of being fully staffed. My five years on the job make me senior to most and seniors get first crack at shift choice. My shift of choice is Monday through Friday, 6AM to whenever. Shifts are twelve hours long but EMS can legally tack on up to four hours as mandatory overtime. After sixteen hours they can only beg us to work longer. An EMT I know will bring a sleeping bag and be with his unit seventy-two hours straight taking naps whenever he can. The suburban cities that ring Louisville don't have this staffing problem for the simple reason that they pay better.

EMTs working overtime don't completely make up for being short staffed. It could mean that instead of arriving on the scene within the national average of eight minutes, it might be ten or twelve. And that could mean the difference between life and death.

Once an EMT earns a paramedic rating, that person finds the grass is greener at hospitals. The hospital work is still hard, but the pay and hours are better.

"Unit 144 ready to rock and roll," Angela said into the radio.

"Unit 144, post to Audubon," came the reply from dispatch. I breathed a sigh of relief. We were being directed to Audubon Hospital in a central, quieter part of town where I could get another cup of coffee and maybe a little shut-eye in the back of the truck before we were sent on a run. The Audubon post wasn't close to any major highways and gun fire in the area was rare. Our job would be to sit in the parking lot, engine running until dispatch called and sent us to help someone.

When you spend a dozen consecutive hours with your partner and share the joy of saving someone's life and the sadness of a person dying as they stare into your eyes, a closeness develops. Those stacks of hours and that closeness can lead to intimacy. And that explains the writing on the bathroom wall at home base, "**EMS** – **E**very **M**edic **S**leeps around." No doubt this goes a long way to explaining the high divorce rate in the profession.

Angela Barton was known as "the psyche whisperer" among EMTs because she can turn on this smooth, café au lait voice that calms and seduces her patients. Had she chosen to be a TV evangelist, she would be quite wealthy. I told Angela all about my week from hell as she drove us to Audubon.

"Well shit, Paxton, I'm so sorry. That skank," she said shaking her head. "You're one of the good guys. You're loyal and faithful and you don't screw around, like everybody else in this outfit."

"Umm," I started.

Angela spun 90 degrees to face me. "What?"

I didn't meet her eyes but felt the heat and anger from her stare. "No way! Jesus Christ on a crutch, can't any of you guys keep it in your pants?" she shouted. Her shoulders slumped, and she turned away from me in disgust.

I closed my eyes and sank into my seat. "I don't think Gwen…"

Angela cut me off, "Knew? You don't think Gwen knew? Is that what I'm gonna hear?" Her hands held a white knuckled choke on the steering wheel. The café au lait was gone, replaced with the bite of bitter, dark roast.

"I've got breaking news for you Paxton Gahl, you dumb shit, your face is a picture worth a thousand words and anybody can read it. It's a good thing you don't tell lies for a living because you'd starve."

The memory of my one and only infidelity came to me unbidden and unwelcome. It had been my first year on the job and I was riding with Pam Eastman. We had put in a busy fourteen hours when we got called to a traffic accident, Code 3.

When we arrived at the scene, the driver of one car, dazed, his face bloodied, was just being helped from his car by passers-by. When he realized where he was and what had happened, he looked in the back seat of his car and became frantic. He yelled, "Ellie, where's Ellie?" A couple of people pointed to a crying baby in the car seat. "No," he yelled. And, again called out, "Ellie," as he frantically looked around the cars.

The discovery of Ellie was announced with a scream of anguish by an elderly man who had joined in the search. He fell to his knees and vomited next to the sidewalk. Pam realized what had happened before I did and took charge. She told people to stay back and signaled for me to stop the father from approaching.

As the story emerged, we learned three-year-old Ellie had pitched a squirming fit when her father had tried to fasten her into her car seat and in frustration, he had given up.

The impact of the crash hurled Ellie through the windshield like a cannonball. Her little body in her pink dance costume was found in some bushes, thirty feet from the crash. They were only two blocks from their home.

The city provides counselors for first responders who see this kind of tragedy in their work, but most of us find no one will understand better than our brothers and sisters in uniform. If soldiers talk about the battles they were in, it is done most freely with other soldiers, not civilians. This is no different. I couldn't even imagine telling Gwen about this car crash.

Pam held it together until we cleared the scene and then she was racked with heaving sobs. Her face transformed from one of the most beautiful I've ever seen to the mug of an English bulldog, all jowly with layers of wrinkles materializing out of nowhere. I hugged her and began to cry myself. One thing led to another.

CHAPTER THREE

Each ambulance has a GPS, and 911 dispatch knows exactly where all the units are all the time. They will send the closest unit with the skill set for the task at hand. The unit numbers have three digits. Unit numbers beginning with a number one indicate there's a paramedic on board. Unit numbers beginning with a two mean both medics are basic EMTs. Our unit was number 144, the paramedic being Angela. It takes an EMT from twelve to eighteen months of additional training to get certified as a paramedic, and I was only halfway through my training. My excuse was that I didn't want to come home and study after working a long shift.

I had managed to down a large cup of black coffee before, "283, see the dancer. Possible broken ankle, 14309 Poplar Level Road, Code 1" came over the radio.

I tuned out the call the moment I heard a unit number that wasn't ours, but Angela sat up like a hound that had just gotten the scent. "That's no dancer, that's a stripper at Teasers," she shouted, throwing the truck into gear. "Hang on, we're jumpin' the run. Can't be two miles from here."

Angela's hope was that in a couple of minutes dispatch would see the little blinking light on their computer screen and notice Unit 144 was, in fact, closer to 14309 Poplar Level Road than Unit 283. We hadn't been sent on this run, but Angela was hoping dispatch would tell us to take it. What dispatch wouldn't know was that our progress to the scene wasn't because traffic was lighter on our route. We would get there first because we were flying with Code 3, lights and siren. Unit 283 was getting there at mule speed as ordered, Code 1, no lights or siren.

Angela and I are both attracted to women. When an attractive woman walks in front of the ambulance at a stop light, our heads turn and go up and down like a couple of bobble heads on the dash. On this day, I would assist her on the drive, keeping an eye out for the deaf and blind who were sure to slow us down, but neither my heart nor my head was in it.

The sugar plums dancing in Angela's head at the prospect of meeting a stripper were dashed before we'd gone a hundred yards. "Unit 144, see the man about a body in the water, Ohio River near Lincoln Memorial, Code 3."

Angela executed a U-turn that tapped the curbs on both sides of the road. We were on our way.

"This could be the guy with the homebuilt plane," I said.

"Whether it is or isn't, there'll be a lot of cops and press. Straighten yourself up, you look like shit. Are your eyes working in tandem yet?"

"I'm fine," I said, running my fingers through my hair.

A week before, a guy in an experimental aircraft he built from a kit in his garage was flying over the river following every bend when he forgot to duck for a high-tension power line running across the river. The plane plunged straight down into the river and quickly disappeared. The river was swollen from a big rain that occurred in the northern Kentucky area and made its way downstream to Louisville en route to the Mississippi. Despite many witnesses and days of searching, neither plane nor pilot had been found.

At Waterfront Park, a statue of Honest Abe sits on a rock mere yards from the mighty Ohio. He sits in all his bronze self, pausing from the book in his hand. He's facing the river and the new billion-dollar bridge named for him. I rested from a jog once at this tranquil spot and tried to imagine the thought process in naming the new bridge. Did the governor come to this park to see the almost completed bridge and say, "What are we gonna call this thing?" It would have taken a governor with the moxie of Lincoln to name the bridge after our hometown hero, Muhammad Ali, and we didn't have a governor like that. The bridge could have been named after the Hill sisters who wrote a birthday song heard all over the world every minute of every day. But if the bridge had to be tagged for a white male, then the governor could not have done better than Edwin Hubble. This later-to-be famous astronomer lived in Louisville and crossed this very river every day to teach school in New Albany, Indiana.

When we arrived, I cut the siren as Angela eased the truck onto the grass. We headed in the direction of a police car parked at the river's edge. TV crews were setting up. I looked for and spotted the lovely Malika Kelly, LMPD PIO, stepping out of her unmarked black van. Sgt. Kelly is the police information officer for Louisville Metro and on call 24/7 to answer questions from the press about any and all police matters. I do love a woman in uniform. I ran my fingers through my hair again.

Malika is on TV, radio, the newspaper and social media all the time because it is her job to liaise with the press and answer all the questions to which they are entitled to have answers.

My feet hit the ground as Angela rolled our truck to a stop. "Have you got a grappling hook?" was the greeting from an excited beat cop who skipped a salutation. "We can't reach the body from the shore." There, among the driftwood and flotsam and jetsam of debris, I spotted a leg. Mingling with the damp, earthy smell of the river was the rank smell of rot.

"No, we don't carry a hook, but Fire is probably on the way." But I looked around and walked to a houseboat parked nearby. "Hello. Anybody on board?" I shouted, knowing no one would have still been inside amid all the flashing lights and racket. The memory of a houseboating weekend had me looking for and spotting a long pole with a small hook attached to the railing of the boat. Aluminum poles with hooks are standard houseboat equipment, perfect for retrieving items and people lost overboard.

The pole wasn't quite long enough, but I was able to use it to float the whole debris pile toward the shore. When I managed to hook a shoelace on a red Nike, we discovered there wasn't a body, but just a leg. It was a hairy, right leg sheared off at the groin. It was white and swollen with a hint of green you don't want to see in a leg. The swollen foot was straining against the laces and the sneaker looked as though it would burst open. "Looks like a towboat got to him first," I said to Angela. The propeller on the towboats pushing barges up and down the Ohio can be six feet in diameter and chopping a body up would amount to less than a hiccup to anyone in the wheelhouse. It was surprising there was this much left.

Behind us Sgt. Kelly, her hand to her face, said "Phew. I never get used to that smell."

In my job, I sometimes encounter the putrid smell of rotting flesh and this smell hadn't gotten pungent until I pulled it close to shore. I was determined not to barf. My gag reflex was, no doubt, more sensitive because of last night's six-pack of Walmart Lite.

Angela distracted me from the smell when she said to Kelly, "Sergeant, it looks like this guy had an artificial hip. That means there will be a serial number."

"And 'presto' we'll have an ID. Thank you, guys," said Sgt. Kelly as she turned and headed to the press corps corralled behind the caution tape.

I started to pull the leg out of the water to 'bag it n' tag it' when Angela stopped me. "Why don't we leave it in the water for the medical examiner," she said. "We'll save ourselves a lot of paperwork." But then she remembered the press and glanced over her shoulder and at all the cameras pointed our way. She winked and said, "What the hell, let's land this carp. Grab a bag," she said, taking the pole from me. I retrieved an industrial trash bag from the truck and Angela made a show of lifting the leg out of the water, pausing as if she were being careful and then letting it settle into the bag I held open.

I was happy to let Angela have the spotlight and traded her the bag for the pole. I rinsed the hook and took the pole back to the houseboat where I noticed what I hadn't before. A light bulb clicked on in my head when I saw the "For Sale" sign in the window.

My apartment was too big, too empty and held too many memories. I had to get out and here before me was the answer. A houseboat on the Ohio River. At the time, I didn't have any plans to throw myself in.

CHAPTER FOUR

At Louisville, the Ohio River is the only thing keeping Indiana from creeping into Kentucky. It's a big job, so it's a good thing the Ohio isn't puny. It has muscle and mastery and every now and then it will remind you who's in charge. But the tourist brochures are exaggerating a bit when they say it's a mile across. That's the kind of mile I want if I ever run a marathon.

I'd drained a brewery or two since the day Gwen left me and I decided that drinking a lot of beer on a houseboat would be even better. After our shift ended and I'd downed a couple of beers, I went exploring along the harbors and coves found off River Road which runs alongside the river. At Limestone Marina I looked for a guy to ask my most basic question. "Do people live on houseboats in Louisville?"

"You bet," said Pete Ford, who was unloading supplies from his car. He looked down on the harbor and added, "Not many. I can think of only three in here who live on theirs year-round. You lookin' for a boat?"

"I'm looking for a new place to live and thinking small. Tiny houses are a thing now, but a small houseboat seems like a better idea."

Ford saw the "Louisville EMS" emblem on my uniform and said, "Come on, give me a hand with this stuff and I'll show you around. Can I buy you a beer?"

"Is a bear Catholic?" I said, perhaps a bit too eager.

Ford was short and solid like a fireplug. With a proud but pudgy finger he pointed to the biggest boat in the marina, "That's mine on the end of the row. Fifty-two feet. Longer than that won't fit in here."

"Ah, the big fish in the small pond," I speculated.

Ford only smiled, pleased with the reference.

Painted across the stern was a name that would produce a groan from everyone who saw it. Ford Pete's Sake. Inside, I set down the load of supplies, and I was looking over the instruments and captain's wheel on Ford's 2007 Jefferson Pilothouse when he approached me carrying a tray like a waiter. With a towel draped over one arm he presented a bomber of ale and two frosted mugs from the freezer. The label read "Pliny the Younger, Russian River Brewing Company."

"I've heard rumors of this," I said, handling the bottle like it was a trophy. "Doesn't it have a high alcohol content?"

"Ten and one quarter per cent and twenty-two ounces of a very fine brew. That's more than I want to take on by myself on a Monday night, but if you'll give me a hand, I'll open 'er up."

"I'm doin' this for you," I said.

Ford poured and only one of us waited for the foam to settle. "Tell me about your boat," I said as I wiped an arm across my upper lip.

"Come on, I'll show you. Two bedrooms, two full baths and one half-bath, fiberglass hull, twin 540hp Cummins diesels and flying bridge. The wife and I have two kids, and we're on the river most weekends in summer."

"What's a flying bridge?"

Ford walked over to the captain's wheel. "It's a pilothouse, I guess you'd say. It's got all the controls you see right here: wheel, throttle, radio, gauges but they're up top. You have a better view up there. It's easier to navigate."

We walked through the kitchen. Granite counter tops, Sub Zero refrigerator, under the cabinet microwave; this was much nicer than my apartment. The decoration theme was 'the beach' and the colors were pink and beige. Seashells were everywhere: seashell candy dishes, soap dishes, vases, picture frames, on the window and shower curtains. The decorator had learned her craft when a castaway on a desert island.

"How far do you go? What's your longest trip?" I asked.

"Madison, Indiana so far. That was a good weekend trip. By car, it's only an hour or so but by boat we make it last most of the day. We dock and walk into town for dinner and stay overnight on the boat. Beautiful town."

Looking at my half-empty glass, I said, "If it wasn't for this, I could probably think of a diplomatic way of asking how much a boat like this costs."

"This one is probably worth 400K, but if you have to ask, you need to know what BOAT stands for: **Break Out Another Thousand**," said Ford pronouncing each word with distinction. He was clearly proud he could **Break**

Out Another Thousand.

"Is there any point in my looking for something in the 50-70K range?" I asked.

"Absolutely. Remember, the two happiest days of a man's life are the day he buys a boat and the day he sells his boat. So, there's always a bargain to be had, just take your time, research and get a marine survey."

"A marine survey?"

"Yeah, you hire a surveyor, a boat expert who looks it over, stem to stern. Like a house inspector in the real estate business," Pete said.

Immediately, I thought of Crunchy. My best friend and I go way back to second grade. We sat across from each other at lunch one day and he introduced me to a type of peanut butter that I'd never seen at our house. I saw him twist two crackers apart to inspect the thick, gooey, brown filling between, and I noticed the uneven bumps. "What's wrong with your peanut butter?" I said.

"It's crunchy peanut butter. Want one?" Cliff Reilly said. That thick gooey bond cemented our long friendship and earned his nickname. Cliff is a self-employed, structural engineer whose typical day could take him anywhere in the city and out. If you were opening a pizza joint on restaurant row in the Highlands and you needed to know if the floors in your 100-year-old building could handle the weight of your new pizza ovens, Cliff was your guy. Want to put a helipad on top of your corporate office tower but it wasn't built for that? Cliff will deliver the bad news when he hands you his bill.

I would ask Crunchy to be my marine surveyor.

As we finished our beers and the tour, Pete walked me to the door.

"How long does it take to get used to this movement from the boat?" I asked.

Pete looked around. "The marina stays pretty calm. I think the movement you're feeling might be coming from that mug in your hand. Look, there's a pretty good restaurant right here in the marina. I'm picking up a pizza to take home to the family. Why don't you get something to eat before you drive home? You don't want one of your co-workers having to scrape you off a tree."

That sobered me up. I'd been on the scene of more DUIs than I could count.

CHAPTER FIVE

By Thursday afternoon, I had put in almost sixty hours at work that week and had earned a three-day weekend. That was both the good news and bad news as it meant I would have a lot of time to dwell on my miserable life. Thirty-six years old, soon to be divorced, living alone in an empty shell of an apartment, and not much to show for my life. My goal for the weekend was to stay sober enough to find a new place to live. The apartment was getting to me. It was too big, too empty and it was too Gwen.

It was time to do some houseboat research, but Gwen had taken the computer and my phone wasn't up to the task. Since I'd had two beers for breakfast, I walked the mile or so to the public library in order to use their computer. As Pete Ford had predicted, there were plenty of boats for sale but there was only one that hooked me.

The one I wanted was a 1970 Kings Craft 34 Coastal Cruiser. It was a beauty at thirty-four feet long and fourteen feet wide with one cabin for sleeping and one bathroom big enough for one person. It had an aluminum hull, a single 224hp Chrysler engine, a Kohler generator, AC and heat. The small galley kitchen was perfect for someone who doesn't cook.

Home from the library, I opened a brew and called Cliff. Without salutation he said, "Pax, how's it goin' buddy?"

"It's great," I lied. "I may have found a new place to live and I could use your help."

He hesitated before he said, "I know you don't need help moving furniture, because there is hardly any left."

Cliff had been at the apartment on the morning Gwen moved out. In hindsight, I realized he had come as a referee anticipating arguments between Gwen and me over our possessions. He hadn't anticipated how drunk and apathetic I had become. In the division of our stuff, my mantra was, "Take it, take it all, I don't care." I had Cliff to thank for what little Gwen left behind.

"I told you about the idea of living on a houseboat and I think I found one. It's at River Park Place Marina." I stumbled a bit before I got that name out. "It's across from Towhead Island. From all the photos and description, it looks perfect for me, but I need an engineer's opinion."

Cliff was a little less guarded. "Alright, I can do that."

Cliff is known for the long pauses he places between thoughts. "Crunchy is crunching the numbers," we used to say in high school. He could also be blunt. "Your speech sounds a little sloppy, I'll drive."

I was surprised. "Yeah. Okay." I thought I had been covering well.

To show I was more on-the-ball than I sounded, I told Cliff, "I called the number in the ad, it was the attorney representing the seller. She told me how to get in and how to start it up."

"Do me a favor; eat some lunch and hold off on the beer for a while. This is a serious investment. I'll pick you up in about two hours. What'd ya say?"

"Right," I said, irritated by the crack about my beer drinking.

I immediately fell asleep on the futon. I wasn't sure if I was woken up by my bladder or Cliff pounding on the door. "Ready?" he said.

I stared at Cliff until I remembered why he was there. "Yes," I said, patting my pockets and looking around the room as I tried to focus my concentration. "Absolutely. Just let me grab a sandwich." I found both peanut butter and jelly! For bread there was one whole wheat heel. I topped it with four stale saltine crackers. I unscrewed the cap, sniffed the milk, then poured it down the drain.

Towhead was the second name for the island that shelters River Park Place Marina. The island was originally named Willow Island but by the mid-1800's the willow trees had all been cut down to fuel the boilers of steamboats. When those steamboats weren't exploding, they were moving a lot of people and products on the Ohio River.

Crunchy and I found the Kings Craft in slip number 26 at the end of a row for boats forty feet long and under. She wore her Sunday best coat of glossy white paint with navy blue Bimini top like a bonnet.

"I think I'm in love," said Crunchy.

"No, no, I need you at your skeptical best," I said. "That's what I would be paying you for if I were paying you."

"In that case, I'll start by telling you a boat is a hole in the water where you pour money."

"Learn that in engineering school?"

"No, but I think it sets the right tone."

"Did you notice the fine print in the invisible contract I didn't hand you since you're not paying me?" Cliff asked.

"I couldn't make it out," I said, playing along.

He pointed to his hand as if it held something, "It says you're out of your frigging mind to spend this much money on something without having an expert look at it. It says, at the very least, you should have it pulled out of the water so I can look at the hull."

"OK, you've fired your warning shot across my bow. I do appreciate your advice. Let's look inside, maybe it's a dump," I said.

Cliff slipped into coveralls before he stepped on board and spent almost no time above deck. He was mostly interested in everything below the waterline. He looked for loose or missing rivets in the hull and for rotted wood. He checked the motor mounts. He had me start the motor and checked the motor mounts again.

The Kings Craft had about three hundred square feet of living space but because there were more windows than walls, it felt bigger. The boat wasn't a dump and I signed the papers and took on my first mortgage.

CHAPTER SIX

The only thing I didn't like about the houseboat was the name painted across the stern. "Bloomers" was painted in block letters that were proportionally too small for the space. It was like the owner wasn't too confident about his name choice. I would have to think of something more appropriate. The boat was the love child of a former bank president named Norman Threadgill. Mr. T had recently departed this life and his grieving widow was getting rid of his toys through the bank's attorney. The attorney, Dorothy, "call me Sarah" Koenig, told me Mrs. Threadgill had never set foot on the boat and had resented it from the day her husband bought it. In an indiscretion I would be reminded of later, Koenig mimicked Mrs. Threadgill. "I never understood why he would want something so small and cramped," Koenig said with a haughty falsetto that told me both why Mr. Threadgill wanted to get away from the Mrs. and what Dorothy, "call me Sarah" Koenig thought of the boss's wife. Neither wife nor attorney knew why Mr. Threadgill had named his boat, Bloomers.

"Mr. T was strictly professional with his staff, I didn't even know he had a boat until after he died," said Koenig.

Mrs. Threadgill ordered Sarah to go through the boat and video the contents so she could decide whether to keep anything. Mrs. T saw nothing she wanted on the video and sold it to me "as is." "As is" meant it came with a set of first-class fishing tackle, some gardening tools, a kitchen stocked with everything I could need, deck chairs with cushions, HD TV, Bose sound system and Norman's toothbrush and dirty underwear. This was a turn-key operation. All I had to supply was my own toothbrush and dirty underwear.

As soon as I took possession, I set about to explore every nook and cranny. And there in the pantry, hidden among the Tupperware containers, I found a small plastic box with dozens of nineteenth century French postcards.

When I saw the photos on the cards were of bored women wearing nothing but bloomers, I decided I wouldn't have to rename my new home after all. I would just frame and hang a postcard or two.

The River Park Place Marina was a bit too upscale for my taste. It is too exposed to the baking summer sun, too busy with pedestrians, and there is too much boat traffic. I dusted off my Catholic heritage and asked to rent a berth at the Knights of Columbus docks on the river. The Knights docks are strictly for summer boating. The Ohio River gets a lot of driftwood and flooding in the fall and winter, and over the cold months the Knights dock isn't a safe place for a boat.

Just before Derby Festival time, around mid-April, the Knights of Columbus boaters converge with drills, hammers and saws. They pitch in to inspect every plank on the dock and replace rotted lumber. Water lines are cleared, and electric lines are run to every slip. A dredge-boat is hired to clean out each slip to a depth of six feet. My Bloomers purchase came to me with two years remaining on the lease of slip #26 on Dock G, so when November rolled around, I would take the boat back to River Park Marina and the protection of Towhead Island. Like the idle rich, I would winter in one place and summer in another.

When I bought Bloomers and secured a mooring at Knights, I was sober enough to know I needed someone with experience at the wheel to help me move the boat to the Knights docks. In Kentucky, anyone over eighteen can operate a boat without a license or any training which is why boating can be dangerous here.

I remember as a teenager going to a dance on the steamboat, the Belle of Louisville, as it lumbered up and down the Ohio. Some kids in a runabout would shoot by us at high speed yelling and acting nuts. Then they must have thought it would be fun to ride the wake of the mighty sternwheeler. The Belle may be slow, but she's three decks high, over 160 feet long and leaves a wake that is nothing to trifle with. The runabout was quickly swamped. All aboard were rescued by more experienced boaters who were alert to the stupidity they were watching. But the runabout went to the bottom, never to be seen again.

My only experience handling a watercraft was a rented canoe on the Blue River in southern Indiana. Gwen and I had gone canoeing with two other couples. The river was unworthy of the name that day as we frequently found ourselves run aground on the shallow stream. When we did have a sufficient amount of water under us, Gwen and I found our paddling of that shiny aluminum canoe was so out of sync that we would crash from one riverbank to the other just like the shiny steel ball in a pinball machine. Maybe I should have read this as an omen.

CHAPTER SEVEN

Still working together in Unit 144, Angela Barton and I got called one day to some condos at the Limestone Marina. Angela and I nodded when we heard the address and the instruction to "see the man" who'd fallen. Mac Preston was an EMS frequent flier and we had seen him a couple of times before.

Eighty-two years of age, Mr. Preston was widowed and retired, or as he told it, thrown out of his own medical supply business by his ungrateful children. Much of Mr. Preston's success was because his sociability got his foot in the door. His success compelled him to buy this gorgeous million-dollar home on a bend in the river where he could see downtown Louisville in the distance to the west and a sexy new billion-dollar bridge to the east. But his lifeblood was people and they were far in the distance in all directions. So about once a month EMS would get a call. Last time Mr. Preston called 911 he said he had chest pain. The time before it was shortness of "air" as he put it. This time he'd said he'd fallen and couldn't get up. This lonely man could have starred in a music video for Paul McCartney's song about Eleanor Rigby.

It took us ten minutes from the call to reach Mac Preston's door where he met us standing upright on his own two feet. We each took an arm and guided him to a chair. He was clearly happy to see Angela again and she fawned over him with that soothing, caring voice of hers that mesmerized Mac and me both. My eyelids had started to droop when Angela turned to me in a voice dripping with honey, "Paxton dear, could you, perhaps, use that device in your hand to check Mr. Preston's blood pressure?"

Angela and I stayed as long as we could and let Mr. Preston talk about anything and everything. He had nothing to say about his fall, if there had really been one. After about twenty minutes, when Mac was looking out the window to show me the Mississippi Queen riverboat making its way downriver, Angela pushed the speak button on her lapel microphone causing mine to squawk.

"That's our cue, I'm afraid we're needed back at our unit Mr. Preston," I said. "You should think about getting rid of those loose throw rugs; they can trip you up."

Angela held it together until we were in the elevator where she bust a gut laughing. "That 'loose throw rug' was an oriental carpet probably worth more than your car."

This all happened on a Friday, and as we left the condo, I stopped at the marina and left a note on the door of the boat, For *d* Pete's Sake. I had been a little too lubricated to think to ask for Pete's phone number last time I was there. The note asked Pete if he could look over my shoulder as co-captain as I drove Bloomers from River Park Marina to Knights.

An hour later, I ignored the vibrating phone in my pocket. Angela and I worked feverishly but in vain on a ten-year-old boy. He had been sitting at his dining room table doing his homework when two men in the street a few doors down decided to settle an argument with gun fire. The boy was struck in the chest and he took his last breath staring at the pencil in his hand that the bullet had splintered before it killed him. His mother screamed with anguish such as I've never heard, clawing at my back as she tried to break free from the officers restraining her. We were all crying. I wanted a beer so badly.

Angela and I were permitted to end our shift early. Minutes after going off duty, I was guzzling down a can of Coors at a gas station a block from base. I sat in my car for twenty minutes eating a bag of chips, wanting to smooth off the buzz just enough to get me home where the refrigerator was well stocked with several six-packs. While I sat in my car I thought about where I could get another beer if I needed it on the fifteen-minute route to my home. Then my phone buzzed again reminding me that I had a message.

Pete Ford's message said he would be glad to help me move my boat in the morning and he laid out the logistical dance we would need to perform for moving one boat, two cars, two marinas and two people around the game board.

When I started the engine on that Saturday morning in mid-June, Pete pointed to the gas gauge. He laughed and said, "Time to introduce you to the neighborhood gas station." Gas pumps are not plentiful on the river which is one of the reasons fuel is about twenty percent more per gallon. The tank held 250 gallons, so a fill-up put quite a dent in my credit card. As the digits spun in a blur on the pump, I decided I needed to think of this vessel more as a house than as a houseboat.

That ride from River Park Marina to Knights taught me that the weekend is not the time to begin learning to drive my boat. As soon as we left the shelter of the marina, boats and waves came from every direction. I felt like I was sixteen, had just gotten my driver's permit and was merging onto the highway at rush-hour. Pete stood at my elbow and in a calm voice, gave instructions.

"Go to the right of the kayak." "Turn into that wake." Then he got inventive, "There's a treeberg, give it a wide berth." Later he explained that ninety percent of an iceberg is underwater, and in the river, what looks like a tree branch may be a whole tree.

We both let out a sigh of relief when Bloomers was safely ensconced in its summer home at the Knights of Columbus dock.

I settled into the life of a river rat. River rats drink a lot. At least I did. There is something about sitting on the upper deck under a Bimini top watching a tow of barges quietly glide by, that calls for a cold brew or six. Weekends were the most liquid. Weekends meant never drinking alone.

Of the two dozen boats at Knights, only two contained permanent residents before I showed up. At one end, there were the Shepards, Celia and Bob, a friendly couple in their late sixties with a beautiful Pluckebaum they had named Glory Days. The name must have referred to the days before they had children because the Shepards' child-rearing experience had been a real trial. They'd had twin sons, and both had been in trouble throughout their youth. Expelled from private Catholic all-boys high school their freshman year, they went on to arrests for vandalizing the same school. They wrecked two cars, collected a DUI apiece and then got into drugs. The Shepards sent their sons to separate rehab facilities where they met their future wives.

Bob and Celia retired the minute they turned sixty-six years old and could collect full Social Security. They put their four-bedroom house in the suburbs on the market and when it sold, they took the proceeds and moved into a tiny one-bedroom apartment while the Arthur Pluckebaum Company custom built their new home.

Glory Days was built with only one bedroom to eliminate the possibility of the sons moving back in with mom and dad when things got rocky. The Shepards fully expected unplanned grandchildren and they wanted to avoid sleepovers at Grandma and Grandpa's house. Glory Days is a custom-built castle. The river serves as a moat around it. Not only could they raise the draw bridge anytime, but they were ready to pull up anchor and flee at a moment's notice. The Shepards' boat was the only one at Knights that was backed into its slip for a quicker get-away.

Representing the other end of the dock, and the extreme, lives a falling down drunk by the name of Richard Bush. Richard bleeds the blue of the University of Kentucky Wildcats. His houseboat, painted UK blue, is a forty-year-old Sumerset named Blue Dick. I don't believe the name on his boat is an enticement when he is trying to get a date, but my wife had just left me so what the hell did I know?

Both Richard and his boat are suffering from neglect. If there is a serious storm, it will be interesting to see which goes to the bottom first, Richard or his "Blue Dick."

Misery loves company and Richard and I spent many hours on the aft deck of his boat drinking. During the day we would sit in the only shade he had outside, that created by the upper deck overhang. His Sumerset had a Bimini top but the dark blue canvas was shredded by age and shaded almost nothing. For after sunset imbibing, we would seek a change of pace; we moved up-top. After I got to know him, he confided that he liked being the end boat on the row because it allowed him to relieve himself into the river from the far side of the boat.

"There is just something about being able to take a piss outdoors. It's freedom, that's what it is," Richard said.

I had to nod in agreement.

"Ya think women feel that way?" he asked.

"I don't know," I said. "Do you know any we could ask?"

Richard Bush is an Iraq war veteran who had little to say about that experience except that it was "fucked up." His only income is a disability check that keeps him "liquid." He takes ownership of his drinking problem and claims it doesn't affect him. "I'm a functioning alcoholic," he said with some pride, "like Vincent Van Gogh and Winston Churchill." When he is not functioning so well, he is apt to repeat this statement several times adding the claim that he is a distant relative of "Uncle Winston." His bookshelf has several biographies of the great man.

As a latecomer to the K of C family, I was assigned one of the two remaining berths right in the middle of the row and the action. On weekends, a fire grate surrounded by lounge chairs on a cleared patch of land directly in front of Bloomers is a popular place to be, even when it's too hot for a fire. And we don't sit there without a beverage. If drinking and partying with my new friends kept me awake, it simply meant I wasn't drinking enough.

CHAPTER EIGHT

My co-workers and I face tragedies every day. The pay is inadequate, and in retirement, we can look forward to dipping into one of the worst-funded state pension plans in the country.

I need my batteries re-charged every day after work, and for that I had the three-legged stool of support: Gwen, jogging and friends. Gwen was gone, beer had replaced jogging, but most of our friends were still my friends. After all, Gwen left town. With legs missing from my stool, I was teetering precariously.

Gwen left a big hole in my life. In days past, I would call her from the truck on some pretense like, "Should I pick up some milk on the way home?" These calls would be made just after we'd ended a run from some terrible accident. I never told Gwen the real reason I was calling was just to hear her voice.

In late June we were posted again to Audubon and had been idling there for forty minutes when we got a call that took us only two hundred yards into a neighborhood park across the street. I was at the wheel and Angela jumped out and ran to the scene while I drove the rig up over the curb and onto the grass, trying to keep up with her. For twelve-year old Nathan Johnson, George Rogers Clark Park was his back yard. He played there every day and in winter when it snowed, this is where he sledded. This day he and his friends were playing Tarzan swinging from a rope tied to a tree branch. The swing took them across the creek that bisected the park. With Nathan at the apex of his arch, the rope slipped its hold around the branch and the unexpected jolt caused him to lose his grip. His friends laughed when he landed on his back in three inches of water, but when he didn't move, they pulled him out of the creek. When I arrived with the truck, Angela, with that smooth, comforting voice, was assuring Nathan he would be all right, the hospital was just over the hill. But it was all for show, for his friends. Nathan was dead. The back of his skull was soft under Angela's fingers and he wasn't breathing. I carried him to the stretcher as police cars and neighbors came running through the woods.

We had gently set the stretcher into the back of the ambulance when we heard a man calling for Nathan. A police officer showed the man into the back of the truck and shut the door. He stared for a long moment at his son and then he looked at me. I found I couldn't speak and only shook my head. As my eyes welled with tears, I longed for a drink.

This had been my park. I had grown up less than a block away. This had been my back yard too. I think I was ten and in school when I learned it had a name other than "the park," that it was named for a revolutionary war hero. My friends and I had collected cuts and scrapes, of course, even a broken arm, but not this.

When our shift ended, I made what was becoming a regular stop, at the gas station near home base for a beer and a bag of chips to hold me over until I got home.

As the summer bore on, the heat and my drinking increased. Up until Gwen left me, I favored a craft beer produced in Lexington, Kentucky called West Sixth. I would buy a six pack and it would take me two weeks to finish it. But after Gwen left, I went for quantity over quality. This was a cost-saving measure. The goal of my drinking had switched from enjoyment to the drowning of sorrows.

In late July, Louisville hit a stretch of 100-degree days. When the forecast called for this slow boil to last awhile, the TV weatherman began to post the day count in the corner of the screen signifying how many days we'd broken the century mark. Then my air conditioner died.

The marine a/c guy was swamped with work so at night I dragged a mattress to the top deck where I slept in my boxer shorts. I drank myself into oblivion every night. In that sorry state, mosquitos had their way with me. After staggering to the rail to relieve myself one night, I had neglected to tuck "Mr. Johnson" away properly. Back on the mattress, I was asleep as soon as my head hit the pillow. When a mosquito sank its lance into the most sensitive skin on my body, drunken reflex took over. I slapped the pest and I knocked my balls into next week. Doubled over in pain, I vomited all over my mattress. Beer vomit, is there anything worse?

CHAPTER NINE

My emotionally downhill ride picked up speed the next day. It was a Tuesday morning and prudence dictated that I should have Coco Puffs instead of Rice Krispies for breakfast because my head was too sensitive for a lot of snaps, crackles and pops. With the first spoonful, I bit down on the inside of my cheek. I froze slack-jawed with my eyes closed, not moving my mouth as I waited for the pain to subside.

In the next couple of weeks, I managed to chomp down on the same spot a couple of more times. I tried to pickle the spot by holding the cheek full of cold beer before swallowing, but that didn't seem to be helping. I put it off as long as I could, but finally it was time to see a doctor.

But I don't really have a doctor; I have a nurse practitioner. And I don't know what to call her. She's not a doctor but she has a lot more letters after her name than RN and calling her "Abby" like she suggested, just seems inadequate. The legend over the pocket of her starched white smock read: "Abagail Grissom Hope, MSN, APRN, FNP-C." Letters in search of an acronym.

The nurse's aide took my vitals and I saw that in the four months since Gwen had left me, my weight, pulse and blood pressure were all up a lot. This was not a surprise, since I hadn't been for a run since the day Gwen executed her coup. And there was the drinking and junk food that had sustained me. I'd gone from a six pack of a local brewery's IPA every two weeks to filling my trunk every week with the cheapest stuff Walmart had in stock.

"So, what's up with you?" Abby asked pointing to my elevated numbers on her tablet.

"I'm not here about that," I said with some heat. "I bit down on the inside of my cheek several weeks ago and it's not healing."

Abby said, "Open up" and after a short look, "It's probably nothing, but I want a dental surgeon to look at it. There's one down the hall unless you've got somebody."

"No, I just have a dentist," I said.

"I'll find out when the dental surgeon can see you," she said curtly as she opened the door.

She returned in a few minutes and said, "You're in luck, Dr. Palmer has had a cancellation and can see you in a half an hour."

"Luck, what is that exactly?" I grumbled.

Ignoring that, Abby said, "Room 370, out the door to the left. By the time you finish the paperwork, he should be ready for you."

"Thanks," I said to my feet. "I'm sorry about earlier; I'm going through some stuff right now."

Her demeanor softened and she said, "When you're ready, we're here to help."

Dr. Palmer was an older guy who made me wonder if Kentucky had an annual Colonel Sanders look-alike contest. I was thinking of the Ernest Hemingway contest they have in Key West every year. The doctor had white hair, a landing strip of a goatee from his lower lip to the bottom of his chin and a moustache. He finished the look with the trademarked, black rimmed glasses of the Colonel.

"I'm guessing you own a white suit," I said.

"Two," he deadpanned.

The doc had distracted me for a minute, but I had taken the afternoon off for this appointment and I didn't want to waste it all on this appointment. As I lay back in the chair, 'Doctor Colonel' looked in my mouth with a magnifying headset and light that could have been stolen from the starship Enterprise. Then he pulled out his cell phone.

"Open wide," he said.

"You mean that fancy gear on your head doesn't have a camera," I asked.

"That would be optional equipment. And this takes a better picture." he said.

When the photo op was over, Doctor Colonel said he agreed with Abby that it was probably nothing, but said due diligence called for a biopsy.

"Can you do your due diligence now or do I need to make an appointment," I said.

"Let's do it, it will just take few minutes," he said.

His assistant materialized from behind me and started to do the prep.

Doctor Colonel produced a syringe and explained he would numb the area and then come back in a few minutes to dig out a tissue sample.

"What about eating and drinking afterward," I asked even though I wasn't thinking of food.

"Don't eat any solid foods for 24 hours. You can have warm soup, applesauce, soft foods, whatever doesn't call for chewing until then. Beverages are fine but watch out for hot coffee," he warned.

All I had in mind was ice cold beer.

It wasn't nothing. Cancer is not nothing. Almost two weeks went by before Doctor Colonel called me at work. My partner Angela and I were between runs just sitting in the ambulance shooting the breeze. Dr. Palmer jumped right in telling me what needed to be done.

I said, "Wait, what? Can I come into your office, like, right now?"

"Sure, that would be fine," he said.

"I'll be there in fifteen minutes," I said. Angela called in to base that we were taking a break and I drove to his office.

Dr. Palmer was all business and the Colonel Sanders glasses were gone. He got right to the point. "You'll have a medical team," he explained. "Oncologist, surgeon, a bunch of folks, but first thing is a CT scan, head to toe."

"You're looking for....," I asked.

"Other cancer," he finished. "We'll get the whole picture and then we can determine what needs to be done."

"Why do I have cancer," as I said the word out loud for the first time, "here," as I pointed to my cheek.

"The number one cause for this type of cancer is tobacco," he said. "Do you now or have you smoked or chewed tobacco," he asked in a way that made me think I was under oath.

"Experimentally as a teenager," I said," but it didn't take."

He shook his head and said, "The number two cause is alcohol, what about that."

"Ah," I said, "that did take."

"There are people who get this type of cancer who don't smoke or drink," he said, "but those two things increase the risk by a lot."

I glanced to my left at the empty seat next to me. This is where Gwen should be. I stayed right next to Gwen when she had her miscarriage. I was next to her and didn't leave her side for two days. I'd held her hand, told her I loved her, and said we would get through this together.

Dr. Palmer said I would get a call the next day to schedule a CT scan. As I left his office, Louisville's three-week heat wave and drought came to an end, and the rain came in a downpour.

I didn't feel like going back to work so I called in a sick rest of the day. The boss didn't give me any lip about taking off in the middle of a shift and that told me Angela had given her a heads up. Angela dropped me at my car, and I headed for Knights. I had no umbrella and it was pouring as I hurried down the thirty-foot steel staircase that ended at the dock. As soon as my rubber soled shoes touched the wooden dock, I slipped and crashed hard to one knee almost toppling into the river.

I shouted "Fuck" into the sky at the top of my lungs. Soaked to the skin by now, I sank to the dock in despair. Oblivious to my surroundings, I don't know how long I sat there before I felt gentle hands grip each of my arms helping me up.

"Come on Paxton, let's get you home," Celia Shepard said from under the hood of her raincoat.

Bob Shepard said, "Careful now, you don't want to be falling into the drink in this monsoon," as I stepped onto the bow of my boat. Had he put emphasis on the word "drink"? They probably thought I was drunk again, and I hadn't had a drink all day, at least not by then.

They hurried on past me to Glory Days just as a clap of thunder drowned out my feeble, "Thanks."

As far as I know, the rain continued all night. Early the next morning I called the EMS medical director, my boss, Brenda Trainor, and told her I had gotten a diagnosis of cancer and I needed to make arrangements with my oncology team. "Paxton, you know the city will provide a therapist to help you get through this," she said. The city urges us to see their counselor after a traumatic event. Angela and I had both gotten calls from them in the last couple of weeks about the crap we'd seen.

"Thanks boss, but my oncology team includes a shrink too," I said not knowing at the time that this was true.

When I told Trainor I needed to stay home to make arrangements for my treatment, planning my "accidental" demise was probably not the arrangement anyone would expect.

CHAPTER TEN

The rain continued with variable intensity throughout the day, but my drinking was "steady as she goes". Through the fog alcohol created in my brain I began to realize the sound of thunder I heard was getting louder. Eventually, it dawned on me, where there was thunder, there must also be lightning. I grabbed an umbrella and bounced from side to side of the galley kitchen until I reached the rear deck. I tried for several minutes to open the umbrella. No matter how hard I pushed the button, it would not pop open. I was too drunk to realize the Velcro strap cinched around the umbrella was the problem. Finally, I held it, un-opened above my head and yelled to the storm, "Light me up mother fucker!"

I had lived on board Bloomers for several months now and had gotten used to the gentle roll of the boat in the waves, but this was my first storm. By evening the wind had picked up and made music as it whistled through the whip antennas of the K of C fleet. As the boat rocked and rolled, books and dishes crashed to the floor of my cabin. The boat's unpredictable movement didn't sit well with my last few beers. I was leaning over the rail to barf when I noticed my stern anchor on the deck at my feet. An idea started to take shape in my pickled brain.

I looked up into the sky, fingers to my mouth in thought like Clarence, the Angel Second Class in "It's a Wonderful Life." I said, "Wait a minute, that's an idea. What do you think? Yes, that just might work." The continuing storm provided all the ingredients I needed.

I tied one end of a twenty-foot rope to a cleat on the stern and the other end to a twenty-pound dumbbell that served as an anchor. I carefully coiled the rope on the deck and took the gate down at the stern. Stepping my right foot into the center of the rope coil, I hefted the anchor in my right hand. I took a goodbye look around and started to swing the anchor in increasing arcs. On the count of three, I threw the anchor as far and as hard as I could into the river. The anchor flew and in an instant the coil tightened around my ankle, jerking me off the slippery deck. I didn't quite make a clean exit because my head caught the edge of the steel deck as the anchor pulled me into the river.

My execution was perfect.

CHAPTER ELEVEN

I saw a bright light at the end of a tunnel. It was unbearably bright. My head was pounding. This can't be death. This is surely worse than death. Then I realized my eyes weren't even open and the "tunnel" was created by my hands being cupped around my eyes. My fingers brushed the gauze bandage wrapped around my head. So, this is what was keeping my head from splitting in two I thought.

I was alive and in a hospital room. A nurse stood at my side. She said, "Good morning."

I briefly opened one eye to look at her but didn't answer. She checked my vitals and looked at my bandage. "Headache?" she asked.

I looked at her with unspoken rage, started to nod but grimaced in pain when I moved my head.

"I can give you acetaminophen," she said.

Recognizing Tylenol when I heard it, I whispered, "Is that all?"

She ignored my question. "The doctor will be in soon; I'll turn off the lights till then."

In the marina, the whole dock and the boats with it rise and fall as the river does but not at the Knights dock. The K of C dock is fixed and if there is flooding, like on that fateful night, the boat's tie-off ropes must have enough slack so the boats stay floating above water even though the docks may be under water. A boat tied firm on the corners with strong rope can find the water rising above the level of the deck. In other words, the boat can sink.

At this point in my life I didn't care about much of anything, but for some reason I wanted people to think my death was an accident. I wanted people to think that I died trying to secure my home in the storm and that I had simply gotten tangled up with the anchor. An accident. Nobody bought it.

My miscalculation had been in thinking no one would be out on the docks in the middle of a multi-cell thunderstorm. For my neighbor, Richard Bush in his boat, Blue Dick, the storm had penetrated his alcoholic fog and put him on alert. A devotee of the Weather Channel, Richard had stopped his drinking when Jim Cantone had come on the air to talk about the storm that was descending on Louisville, Kentucky. Mr. Bush was retired Army and an Iraq War veteran, and he was aware his boat was barely seaworthy. He'd pulled himself together and turned down the spigot on the liquor flow so that his intoxication was strictly at maintenance level. Mr. Bush was the one who called the Shepards at the other end of the dock and suggested that every half hour they leave their boats and walk toward each other on the dock checking each boat, loosing lines and checking knots along the way; meeting in the middle at my boat, Bloomers.

It was Richard Bush who caught a glimpse of me in the darkness and downpour as I threw my anchor. He heard the dull "clunk" as my head hit the deck. It was Richard Bush who realized I was still attached to the anchor rope, out of sight, under the muddy chop of the Ohio. It was Richard Bush who pulled me out, turned me on my stomach and started CPR the old-fashioned way of rocking forward, his hands pressed against my back and pulling my elbows toward my head as he rocked back. It worked and he saved my miserable life.

By the time I woke up in the hospital, the verdict was in. I was severely depressed and had tried to kill myself. I didn't even get an "A" for creativity.

I was assigned a psychiatrist by the name of Dr. Karen Newman. I hadn't asked for a psychiatrist, but it was clear I wasn't going anywhere until I saw one. Since I was a guest of University Hospital and both Abby, my nurse practitioner and Dr. Palmer, the dental surgeon who had delivered my cancer verdict, were both affiliated with that hospital, Newman had access to all my records. It was on day two of my stay in the hospital that I met Newman, and by then she had the goods on me. I didn't care.

Because of the storm and my drinking, Cliff had apparently stopped by Knights to check on me just as the ambulance was tearing away, Code 3. He had come to the hospital, but they had explained that I wouldn't be allowed any visitors for a while. I didn't care. My condition was given as "satisfactory." I didn't care.

Dr. Newman explained that my brother, my only close relative, had rushed in from his home in Covington, Kentucky, a suburb of Cincinnati, Ohio when he'd heard I'd almost drowned. Phillip told her about my divorce and how he hadn't talked to me since, when my speech wasn't slurred. Phillip owned a small lawn care company and had two kids. It would have been difficult for him to get away this time of the year and drive over 100 miles to see me. After Newman had talked to Phillip, she sent him home without seeing me. I didn't care.

As it turns out, my neighbors at K of C had had a meeting and the Shepards had hand delivered a letter to Dr. Newman. The letter revealed my drinking and obvious depression. I didn't care.

Of course, everybody in the EMS family got the news in short order, as well as many of the cops in the city since I had met a lot of them. Dr. Newman told me that she had sent my boss and three of my co-workers away too. "You seem to have a lot of people who care about you," she said. My face was blank when I looked at her because I didn't care.

Dr. Newman explained that she thought the best course of treatment for me was ECT or electroconvulsive therapy; shock treatments. I told her I didn't care.

CHAPTER TWELVE

"So how do you feel?" said the woman hovering over me when I opened my eyes. She was probably in her late forties, with short brown hair. I looked down at her chest where her name was embroidered over the pocket.

"Dr. Newman," I read. "You look familiar."

"You had an ECT yesterday and short-term memory loss is a side effect," she said.

"E..C.., oh the shock treatment," I said with interest, "how did it go?"

She smiled and said, "That's what I'm asking you. How do you feel?"

I sat up in the bed and did an assessment touching my hands to my head, chest and thighs. I must have smiled because the corners of Dr. Newman's mouth curled up as she looked at me. After a couple of beats, I said, "All I can think of are clichés like: a great weight has been lifted off me; I'm as fit as a fiddle; all's well that ends well; an idle mind is the devil's playground; any port in a storm......"

Newman held up both hands in a 'stop' gesture and laughed. "You've been asleep for almost ten hours," she said looking at her computer tablet. "I'll be back to see you in the morning. Do you need anything?"

"Just food; I'm starving," I said.

A nurse I hadn't seen before heard this as he walked in and said, "Dinner is on its way," as he tapped on his tablet.

Dr. Newman returned in the morning just as I was hoovering in the last crumb from my breakfast. When she finished looking at my eyes with her pin light and checking the gash on the back of my head, I asked, "Hey Doc, how do these ECTs work exactly?"

"Well, in fact, nobody knows for sure. There is evidence that certain brain chemicals react to severe depression. We know that electroconvulsive therapy can change the metabolism of the brain in certain areas that are affected by depression," she said.

I stared as she explained that when she was in medical school the primary treatment for a patient with severe depression was talk therapy. That was tried for several weeks and if that didn't work, drugs were tried. "But Prozac and Zoloft can take weeks to kick in and, frankly, I didn't think you had weeks."

Dr. Newman didn't mention that, these days, insurance companies don't want to pay for weeks of talk therapy sessions, so drug therapy is the first course of action.

"You clearly didn't care what we did to you and you did not have a power of attorney, so a health care surrogate was appointed," she added.

Newman asked a series of questions, including, "and who is the president?"

"Are you trying to make me depressed again? We'll just call him number 45," I said.

The Q&A session lasted five minutes, then Dr. Newman stared at me for a moment and came to a decision.

"I had planned more ECTs for you, up to seven more, but I think in light of your vast improvement and the fact that you'll be around the hospital while your cancer is treated, I'm going to send you home," she said. "Your electronic record," she said pointing to her tablet, "will follow you around from oncologist to surgeon and I'll text you for appointments to see me occasionally as our schedules coincide. If you're not sick of all of us at the hospital inside a month then another ECT will be warranted," she joked.

CHAPTER THIRTEEN

When I'd taken my dive into the river, I had only been wearing boxer shorts, and at the hospital they had been tossed in the trash. I mentioned this to Dr. Newman as she was signing my discharge papers, and she asked a hospital volunteer to go to the emergency psych department where the hospital keeps a closet of used clothing for just such emergencies.

With no money for a taxi or phone for an Uber driver, I called Cliff to give me a ride home. I had a lot of people to call, to both apologize to and to thank, but Cliff's was the only number besides Gwen's that I knew from memory. It was apparent the ECT hadn't hurt this long-term memory. Cliff, not recognizing the number on his screen answered in his business voice, "Reilly Engineering."

"Cliff, it's Paxton," I said.

Cliff's reply was a beat off and guarded. "Pax. So, they're letting you use the phone?"

Through my friend's lack of enthusiasm, I sensed his disappointment in me. "How are you?" he said.

"Hey man, I'm sorry about all this. The doc thinks there was a chemical imbalance in my brain. She gave me a shock treatment, an ECT, and it worked. The cancer will take longer but they're sending me home."

"No shit? That's fantastic, when?"

"Now," I said, "Or as soon as they find me some clothes."

"I can be there in thirty minutes," he said.

The hospital volunteer came back from emergency psych with shorts, a tee shirt and flip flops. As a volunteer, she wasn't required to wear the sexless hospital scrubs of the staff. She wore black tights and a snug red blouse with a name tag that was tilted to follow the plunging "V" of her neckline. Her name, written in cursive, was tiny, so I had to turn my head at an angle and stare to read it. "Verdana?" I asked. "Were you named after a font?"

"Verna is my given name," she said with a frown, "after a great grandmother, but I'm looking to replace it. What do you think?" she asked.

"I think you're not sold on it yourself. Look how small you wrote it," I said glancing at her cleavage again.

"Yeah, maybe you're right; I'll keep trying," she said.

Verna hand me the clothes and with a twinkle in her eye, she said "Looks like you're goin' commando."

As I stood there wearing nothing but a thin, ventilated gown in front of this beautiful, flirty woman, I was discovering what huge quantities of alcohol had done to my libido. I was DOA below the waist. I knew this was a side effect of too much booze. I don't think even Viagra could have revived me. It was time for me to get my shit together.

"That's fine," I said taking the offered clothes. "Used clothes I like, but I draw the line at used underwear. Thank you, Verna."

When he pulled up in front of the hospital, Cliff got out of the car and came around and wrapped me in a bone crushing hug. A first for us. Neither of us attempted to speak until we were two blocks from the hospital.

"Buy your lunch?" I said, clearing my throat.

"Sounds great," Cliff said.

"Loan me some money?" I said.

"How about Mayan Café in Nulu. That's close." he said.

"Money is no object," I said, waving an imperial hand.

We turned onto Market and headed east as Cliff gave me an update on a 15,000-square-foot house he'd been working on with an architect. "All five of the bathrooms are each bigger than Bloomers," he said with a laugh. Cliff had run into a major problem, which was that the architect, Gracie Atwood, was flirting with him. She thought they would need to discuss the project "over dinner." But Cliff was in love with Teresa Cooper. He didn't want to jeopardize that relationship, or the house project by turning down Atwood's dinner invite. Cliff was excited about the project because he was hoping to meet the owner of the house, an international best-selling author who was working her way through the alphabet with her series of private eye novels.

I was concentrating on Cliff's conundrum when we passed an old bank building. The hundred-year-old building used to be the German Security Bank. The building is of Greek revival style with three-story tall limestone pillars and a beautiful, six-foot diameter, round, stainless steel bank vault door. Louisville had a lot of German emigrants, but during World War I, the bankers thought it prudent to drop "German" from the name. There were many German businesses and streets with German names that were changed during the war. The bank had long since departed and the current incarnation for the building was a billiards hall. Calling the place "The Bank Shot" must have been too obvious for the pessimistic owners who chose to call it "The Scratch Shot."

As we drove by, I couldn't take my eyes off the place and turned in my seat to stare. I had the strangest sensation. A white man named Harry Lampton was savagely beating a black man named Charles Piedmont with a pool cue. I sat in the passenger seat of Cliff's car with no view inside the building, yet I knew this with absolute certainty. I visualized telling Cliff. Then I visualized Cliff saying, "Uh huh," as he did a U-turn taking me back to the hospital. I visualized him telling the attendant in emergency psych, "I think this one needs a little more work."

For the first time in my life, I had cause to worry about my own sanity. I'd been floating several inches off the ground ever since my ECT but now I was firmly earthbound and carrying a thirty-pound pack on my shoulders.

"Is some woman walking topless or do you find my problems boring?" Cliff asked.

"Huh,… no,… sorry; although your problems would be boring compared to a woman walking topless down Market Street," I said, trying to re-focus.

After lunch, Cliff dropped me at the K of C, but refused to wait while I went to my boat for the funds to reimburse him for lunch.

I spent the afternoon cleaning up Bloomers which included pouring a half a case of beer down the drain. I also steeled myself for a visit to Richard Bush and the Shepards.

As soon as I saw Richard and hailed him, he began to apologize! "Hey man, I thought it was an accident. I didn't know you were trying to off yourself. I wouldn't interfere with somethin' like that. I don't think I would anyhow," he said looking at his feet for confirmation. He was sitting on his back deck in the shade watching a barge 100 yards long quietly glide by when I joined him. He held a bottle of beer in a zippered U of K beer cozy. He pointed to the bottle and raised his eyebrows in a silent question.

"No thanks," I said settling into the deck chair next to his. "I seemed to have lost my taste for the stuff." I looked at my own feet for further prompting. "You did the right thing pulling me out of the river, Richard. I will be grateful forever to you for saving my life. I don't see how I can ever pay you back. Thank you."

Richard Bush nodded once. "Now I'm remembering a story I read about suicides off the Golden Gate bridge," he said. "Very few survive the fall but of the ones that do, almost all of 'em said they regretted it as soon as they stepped into space."

"Well," I said, consulting with my feet again, "I didn't learn that quickly. In fact, it took a shock treatment to get me squared away. But I'm back; it's like my stars have been re-aligned." The scene at The Scratch Shot flashed through my mind, but I shook it off.

I grabbed Richard's free hand in both of mine and shook it. "Thanks man."

The Shepards weren't home, so I left a long note of apology and thanks on the door of their boat. Then I made a very difficult call to my brother Phillip in

Covington. I told him about the ECT and gave him an update on my cancer treatment. The burly, gruff Phillip cried. Both of our parents had died of cancer. "I was all set to come down there and kick your sorry ass," he said. "So, think of it like this, cancer saved you from an ass kickin'."

"I need to get that done up in needlepoint and framed on my wall," I said.

Phil came back with, "The folks down at Gilda's Club would be very proud." As teenagers, Phil and I sat in on cancer support sessions at Gilda's when our parents were being treated for cancer. The club was formed nationwide for the Saturday Night Live comedian, Gilda Radner, who had died of cancer.

Phil and I knew there are all kinds of cancers, some worse than others and we knew that, unlike us, our parents each smoked a pack of cigarettes a day until they couldn't. We agreed to the impossible; we wouldn't worry about this until we got the CT scan results. We promised to talk several times a week.

I turned the TV on and pressed mute while I looked at two text messages on my phone. The messages — my CT scan was scheduled for tomorrow at 8 AM and Dr. Newman wanted to see me at 9.

When I looked backed to the TV, The Scratch Shot pool hall was on the screen. I jumped for the remote and fumbled to unmute the sound. An EMS unit was pulling away in a Code 3, all lights and sirens. ".....according to Police Information Officer Malika Kelly. Please contact Louisville Metro if you have any information on the whereabouts of Mr. Lampton."

CHAPTER FOURTEEN

The text message from Cliff read, "Brunch? 9AM. At TC's."

TC was a little treasure Crunchy had met online named Teresa Cooper. She was smart and sophisticated and Crunchy had upped his game for her. I realized how serious he was about this woman when the morning after their first date he'd gone out and bought coasters for his coffee table. But there was something else I couldn't put my finger on yet. Was he combing his hair a different way, or dressing better, had my best friend always had a moustache? Cliff had been very casual in every other relationship he'd had, but he seemed to be putting some serious effort into Teresa. He'd even asked me to call him Cliff around Teresa and her children, and somehow, I don't think that was her idea. She was divorced and had two kids who were approaching double digits in age.

Gwen and I had been out with Teresa and Cliff just once and the women hadn't hit it off. We had picked up Teresa and Cliff at her house. Dinner and a movie were on the agenda. I had grown lazy in social situations with Gwen present because she could hold up our end of a conversation for both of us. I was sort of the color commentator while she did the play-by-play work. But she had gotten so quiet throughout dinner that night it was a relief to get into the movie theater where we couldn't talk. Later at home, I asked her if she was alright. She said she was fine but when I awoke at three AM, I found her side of the bed was empty.

Sudden clarity struck me right between the eyes. Teresa had a beautiful house, two children and a boyfriend with his own thriving business. Gwen had an old apartment, a miscarriage and, well, me. It was past time for us to sit down together and talk about our future. But we didn't. Gwen's pregnancy that first year had been an accident. Both of us were upset with the miscarriage but I must admit, I was also a little relieved. I didn't voice my relief and, if she had it, neither did Gwen. Wedding plans were in full swing and we took no time to grieve.

Had double dating with Cliff and Teresa awakened a desire in Gwen for kids and a big house in the suburbs? It hadn't done that for me. I felt about kids like I did about a vacation condo at the beach. I preferred to rent one when it suited. I could skip over the whole parent thing and go right to the grandparent stereotype. I was all for baby-sitting nieces and nephews from time to time, but in practice, it only happened twice. The nieces, no nephews, came from my side of the family since Gwen was an only child. She and I had given my brother Phillip and his wife Cindy long weekends away a couple of times when their girls were little. Phillip and Cindy made trips to landscaping trade shows and as the girls and the business grew, they made the trade show an annual family business expense to escape Cincinnati winters.

So, on the Sunday morning after my ECT, I was delighted to find the text message, "Brunch? 9AM. At TC's," when I woke. It was from Cliff inviting me to a home-cooked brunch. The delight part didn't register until it hit me that Teresa Cooper was in the kitchen. Cliff's cooking skills are right up there with mine, so my immediate reaction to the invitation was alarm. I replied to his text with, "Yes please" and he wrote back to say come ahead.

Cliff's house was in the Highlands, but it was up for sale. He was living with Teresa in a part of town that Gwen and I had dubbed, Waylo. Waylo, was the best we could make of WWALOH for Why Would Anybody Live Out Here. The house was in the eastern part of the city. My main objection to Waylo is the traffic; it's merely bad most times but at rush hour it teeters between gridlocked and treacherous.

I thought Teresa was great, but I found her neighborhood a bit creepy. It was all patio homes with attached two-car garages, so you never had to go outside. No trashcans, no litter, and sidewalks where no people walked. Angela and I had an emergency run out here once for what she refers to as "fall down, go boom," and we noticed a familiar and disgusting smell as soon as we got out of the ambulance. While she tended the older gentleman who'd fallen in his bathroom, I stepped up on a lawn chair by the tall privacy fence and looked next door to find what was left of a woman sitting on her back porch. A large black bird stood on her shoulder. She'd died of a heart-attack a week before. The neighborhood gave me the creeps.

One of Teresa's sons met me at the front door. I mentally flipped a coin and said, "Liam. How's it goin' man?"

"We're having waffles," was his reply, so I must have gotten his name right.

"Wait a minute, I heard omelets were on the menu."

"That's for the grown-ups."

"What? You short people get all the good food; what kind of deal is that?"

Liam led me to the kitchen where Chef Teresa was aproned up and orchestrating a grand meal with a spatula in each hand.

I said, "Thanks for having me Teresa, I'm so relieved Crunch, I mean Cliff's not cooking."

I leaned in to peck her on the cheek and she turned to give me a big bosomy hug instead. Since my suicide attempt, the women I know had been doing this. And I don't mind.

"You'll find the boys on the deck. Tell them brunch is served in ten minutes."

Cliff sat at a picnic table holding a set of instructions with very small print. Liam and Noah sat on the other side of the table looking through dozens of parts of some kind of model plane.

"Okay, next find four motor mounts. They look like this," Cliff said pointing to a picture in the instructions.

"Hey, what'ch building," I asked.

"Cliff bought a drone with a camera and we're helping him put it together," Noah said.

"No way; anybody can see you've had a crash and you're trying to glue this thing back together," I said teasing the boys.

"No, it's a kit," said Liam laughing. "It came this way, silly."

"Well ok, if that's your story; but I can see you're not going to be finished before your mom rings the dinner bell, so be ready."

"What's a dinner bell," said Noah.

Cliff spoke up, "It's from the old days back when the cook used to ring a bell for the farm hands to let them know they should come in from the fields because it was time to eat. Back then, most people lived on farms. The main meal was in the middle of the day and they called it dinner.

"So, this looks like a good place to stop. Liam, why don't you plug in the batteries so they'll be charged and ready to go after we eat, or rather after we finish the dishes."

"Aww, come on Cliff, mom can do dishes," said Noah.

"She can but she's not gonna. How long do you think it will take to do the dishes?"

"It'll take too long," Liam whined.

"Ok, I'll tell you what. We'll all make a guess at how long it will take to do the dishes and whoever gets closest to the correct time will get first crack at flying the drone," said Cliff. He tore off three scraps from the French version of the drone assembly instructions. "Write your guess on these pieces of paper along with your name and give them to Paxton. He will be the judge and the decision of the judge will be final. No argument."

After a western omelet, homemade biscuits, a waffle, orange juice and coffee, I was so full I had trouble accessing my pants pocket to pull out my phone. As time keeper, I would need the stop-watch function on my phone. During the meal, Cliff and the boys had talked strategy for dishwashing. Cliff would wash and the boys would clear the table and dry.

"On your mark…get set…go," I said.

I guess it was no surprise that the engineer won, with a guess of seventeen minutes. Liam, the ten-year-old, guessed twenty-five minutes and Noah, who was eight, knew it would take forever, but settled on an hour. The room was ship-shape in nineteen minutes.

I hung around a while talking with Teresa about nothing of importance as Cliff and the boys assembled the drone. I finally made my excuses about needing to do some imaginary boat maintenance and left. I was happy for my friend because he looked like a perfect fit in this family, like he'd been there all along. On the other hand, I was a third wheel, the single guy at a party of couples whose blind date was a no show. I had the urge to buy a six-pack of beer and go sit on my boat. Then, stopped in my car at a light as I made my way out of Waylo, I glimpsed my future. Here was a man, at least in his sixties, gray hair, a week's worth of a spotty beard, staggering, sometimes on, sometimes off the sidewalk. His quarry was a bench. He sat hard, catching only six inches of the four-foot-long bench, righted himself, and pulled a bottle from his pocket.

I stared until a chorus of car horns brought me back to the present. I sat up a little straighter and drove to the station to see if I could pick up some overtime.

CHAPTER FIFTEEN

The next morning, I had my picture taken. A computed tomography or CT scan is a fancy X ray. Mine got even fancier; I had a CT with contrast. I lay down on a narrow table and the technician asked if I wanted a blanket. I was glad I declined because next came an IV in my arm, and when the spigot was turned on, I could feel heat from the contrast as it flowed through my veins. The heat started at the top of my head and spread down past my ears to my shoulders. It was like the hottest blush I've ever had. The contrast material blocks the X rays, making the blood vessels appear white on the scan.

I lay still as the machine slowly rolled me in through the center of this large white donut that is the CT scanner. The scan covered me from the top of my head to my crotch and was over in a few minutes, just as I was starting to nod off.

The meetings with Dr. Newman would become routine as she assessed my mental condition by engaging me in conversation and asking questions. I had no intention of telling her about my "vision" of the fight at The Scratch Shot, and I feared she would sense that I was holding something back. But Newman was focused on looking for depression and any indication that I might harm myself again. She found no cause for concern on that front.

Rather than sit around and worry that the CT scan would show my body was riddled with cancer, I called Brenda, my boss and asked if she had some work for me. "Yep, Paxton, in fact I've got John Cobbs riding with Angela Barton right now and we don't need two paramedics in the same truck. When can you be here?"

I met the truck at base station and after a lot of welcoming pats on the back by my EMS family and a long hug by Angela, we got in the truck.

Our beat this day was downtown, so we headed for our favorite post position. The problem with the downtown post is the number of people who come up to the truck wanting something. I guess they see the City of Louisville logo and they think it should be a city service for us to give a ride, or money. Once a guy in a nice suit and carrying a leather shoulder bag asked for a band-aid and I said, "Sure, where are you injured."

He admitted he wasn't injured at the moment but wanted one "just-in-case." I just stared at him until he said, "Unless there's a drug store around here."

I pointed down the street and said, "Two blocks."

Our favorite spot for a downtown post is the parking lot for Joe's Crab Shack, right down at the river's edge. The parking attendant in his booth waves us through and we park along-side the building, ready to roll.

On the day of my return to work, we didn't have long to wait.

"Unit 144, The Naked Man now appearing at 4th and Broadway, Code 2." Angela and I groaned at the same time. Naked people are not unusual in our business. Men or women, most of the time they're under the influence of something. We can guess what that something is, but we never know for certain until the ER does a urine screen. Naked men are a bigger challenge than women because they may discover their penis when naked and decide to entertain themselves.

Every EMS unit in town had met 'The Naked Man' by now. For the record, in the first EMS encounter with naked man, he wasn't naked, but was wearing an Indiana University baseball cap. Naked man couldn't tell us his name, so he was named by an EMT crew. They named him 'Mike Pence,' because the Vice President was governor of Indiana at the time. Naming him Mike Pence on the official record gave him more dignity then being just another "John Doe" followed by a number. One of the regulars we see downtown pulling a wheeled suitcase is known only as Jane Doe 39.

We eventually learned that naked man Pence perfected his strip act in Indianapolis where the hospital there treated him, then sent him on his way with a Trailways bus ticket, suggesting he would fare better in a warmer climate. A free bus ticket is the solution some cities have as a way of handling the homeless and mentally disturbed.

We knew Mr. Pence would be needing a ride to the emergency psych unit at University Hospital. Once there they would try to get him to take his medication, give him a shower and some clothes, a little something to eat and send him on his way.

"Nobody will be jumpin' this run," Angela said rather mournfully. From a half a block away, we could see Mr. Pence gesticulating wildly.

"Is he doing the YMCA dance?" I asked. He appeared to be performing the song that's become a standard at wedding receptions. Standing atop a park bench his bare ass to the intersection, his audience was six rows deep, mostly black and white, but there was also red, yellow and blue. The audience was made up entirely of shiny new Cadillacs belonging to the dealership on that corner.

Mike Pence was probably in his thirties, of mixed race, at six-foot-four and 300 pounds, he was a gentle giant. A Louisville Metro cop was there when we arrived and had his hand on his holstered taser. Jumping from the truck, Angela said, "Officer, we've got this." I grabbed a sheet from the truck while Angela began her calming magic.

From years of experience, we knew that what Mr. Pence wanted was a bath. In this heat he would go a couple of weeks, sweating and sleeping rough, probably at a nearby highway underpass. He would get to smelling so bad his homeless colleagues would begin to harass him. So, he would throw off all his clothes and wait for help to arrive.

At University Hospital, our favorite nurse, Kathy Cavanaugh was on duty. Thirty years on the job as a psych nurse and she's seen it all. Her patients were all compromised in some way. Most are under the influence of drugs or alcohol, and are a danger to themselves or others. The patient's drug of choice will usually show up in a urine screen, but the methamphetamine users are easy to spot. They are skinny, with rotting teeth, acne and pock skin and they always believe someone is chasing them. Some of her patients come by several days every week voluntarily. Some are brought in by police on mental inquest warrants obtained by a family member at wit's end. Many curse her and call her the vilest names. Some, she knows, had killed people. Some threaten to kill her. Some, like Mike Pence, just want a kind word and a shower.

Cavanaugh had seen Pence many times and didn't need to pull up his chart to be reminded of his case.

"Hi Mike, how ya' doin today? Why don't we get you a shower," Cavanaugh said as she took him by the arm and led him away.

There are always three security guards in the ER and Angela and I were shooting the breeze with them when I saw in my peripheral vision the flash of a knife in the waiting room.

"Hey, he stabbed her," I shouted as I ran to the room, two of the guards and Angela behind me.

If you're going to get stabbed, I guess only an operating room would be a better place. Guards had the man, Gerald Matthews, hog-tied in seconds and doctors and nurses had whisked his pregnant wife, Glenda, away in no time.

But then, as Angela and I headed out to our truck, I realized the waiting room where the stabbing took place couldn't be seen from where I saw it. I did a doubletake and looked back in that direction to check for a security monitor or reflection, anything that would explain what just happened.

I realized I had a bigger problem. How did I know their names? How did I know the names Glenda and Gerald Matthews? Gerald had the right half of his head shaved to show a skull and cross-bones tattoo. A skull on his skull. The left half of his head sported a neatly cut, quarter inch of thick, green hair. This is not someone quickly forgotten.

Not wanting to let on to what had just really happened and risk a trip to the funny farm, I hustled away from the hospital to our truck, hoping Angela would hurry away too before she got suspicious of the obstructed view of the waiting room.

"Whoa, what's your hurry, Hoss?" asked Angela when she got in the passenger seat.

"It's lunch time and I'm starving," I said trying at nonchalance. "Hey, tell me something. Dr. Newman, the shrink who did my ECT, told me I might have some short-term memory loss; have we met that happy couple back there before?"

"Hell no. And I have to say, I haven't been pregnant, but I don't think underwear is completely out of line in her condition, ya know?"

CHAPTER SIXTEEN

At 8 the next morning at our post downtown, my phone rang. Caller ID read, "Morgan."

"Oncologist," I said to Angela as I answered the phone.

"This is Pax."

"The CT scan was negative," she said without preamble. "We found no other suspicious masses."

As I let out a long exhale, she continued, "Now I'll say hello. I thought you'd like the good news first."

"Well done. And thank you," I said as I gave Angela a thumb's-up.

I squeezed my eyes shut and took another deep breath as I let the news sink in. It was the oddest feeling. I had cancer, yes, but I knew it was only in one spot. Who else could say that? Angela, here, sitting next to me could have breast cancer or brain or lung cancer and not know it. I was a cancer patient stretching for a life preserver, I suppose, but in that moment, I *knew* I didn't have cancer anywhere else.

I had met Dr. Rebecca Morgan only once, at University Hospital. I had been put in a room and then the parade started: one at a time there had been: an oncologist, a surgeon, a social worker, a radiologist, a nurse, two "fellows" and a partridge in a pear tree.

"So, Dr. Morgan, when can I get this thing cut out of me?"

"Dr. Monohan's office will give you a call today or tomorrow, I should think, and schedule you for surgery."

CHAPTER SEVENTEEN

I gasped as I bolted upright in my seat, eyes wide open. Angela, next to me in the truck, didn't notice because she had juiced-up the volume on the oldies radio station we were listening to. The Beatles had her trying to twist and shout while strapped in her seat.

A security guard named Cynthia Rodriguez had just been shot by Joel Inman at a bank 100 yards from where we sat at our Audubon post. The problem was I knew this but hadn't seen it. This was just like The Scratch Shot beating. In my mind there was a flash and the scene was seared into my brain.

I was desperate to throw the truck into drive, hit the lights and siren and get to that bank that stood just out of sight, up the road. I kept a white knuckled grip on the steering wheel as I waited for the call from dispatch. To myself, I tried out an alternative. "Hey, Angela, I have a feeling a security guard was just shot at that Chambers bank at the top of the hill. I think she was hit in the shoulder and it looks pretty bad. How about we go patch her up?" Instead, I put the truck in gear and pulled away. "I need a Panera snack," I shouted over the music.

Her, "replacing your beer gut with a pastry gut," sounded more like a statement than a question.

"Unit 144, shots fired, Chambers bank, Poplar Level and Hess, Code 3. Wait for the cops 144."

I was making my way to Panera and the Chambers Bank next door to it, when my eyes followed Joel Inman driving a ubiquitous, silver Camry going in the opposite direction. "Get that plate number," I shouted.

Like many EMTs, Angela had started as a medic in the Army and with that tone in my voice her training kicked in and she didn't hesitate to write the number down on the dash post-it pad.

"What's this for," she said after she'd recorded the car's make and color too. "He was wearing a mask."

Angela grabbed the microphone. "Dispatch, we've got a possible make and model of the get-away car."

At the bank, an employee in the trademark blue bank shirt was waving frantically for us to hurry as we pulled into the bank parking lot. We could hear police sirens, but we didn't wait for the cops. With the trauma bag on the stretcher, we ran inside.

The guard was right inside the door lying on the floor with bank employees huddled round her, one holding a softball size clutch of paper towels to her shoulder another sliding a towel under her head. As Angela peeled back the paper towels, I ripped open some combat gauze. The gauze contains chemicals that speed coagulation and help the blood to clot. Without taking her eyes off the wound, Angela reached an open palm in my direction and I gave her the gauze. Kneeling in a growing puddle of blood, she spoke to the guard in that soothing, calming voice as she stopped the bleeding, "You're going to be all right; this isn't as bad as it feels right now. The hospital is only two blocks away. You will be fine." Everybody's blood pressure dropped when Angela turned on that voice.

I put an oxygen mask over the guard's nose and mouth. "Cynthia, this will make it easier to breath," I said. "And we'll want to start an IV before we take you to the hospital." What I didn't tell her was that we were doing this because we expected her to go into shock due to the amount of blood she'd lost.

"Did you know her?" Angela nodded in the direction of the room where we'd just delivered our patient to the ER at Audubon Hospital.

"The guard?" I said, eyebrows arching. "No. Why do you ask?"

"You called her Cynthia. How did you know her name?"

"I don't know, name-tag, I guess."

"Didn't have one," Angela said.

I tried on a perplexed look to cover the 'oh, shit' look that was forming on my face. "Someone must have said her name then. How else would I know?"

I was beginning to wonder if Angela was getting suspicious of me or had been told to keep an eye on me by Brenda, our boss. For one thing, her usual morning greeting to me had changed. Before my dive into the river, her cheery "good morning" had never been in English. It was always *guten morgan, buenos dias, bonjour* or who knows what. With Google at her fingertips, I could only guess at the language most of the time, although I knew what she was saying. But after the suicide attempt, it was, "How're ya feelin, this mornin'?" Before the attempt, we could sit for long spells in companionable silence as we waited for our next run. Now those silences would be interrupted by, "You doin' alright?" I guess I had this extra scrutiny coming. But I saw a clear downside to mentioning that I'd just had a vision.

Louisville police P.I.O. Sgt. Malika Kelly found me in the Audubon ER cafeteria getting coffee shortly after we delivered Cynthia Rodriguez. Angela was in the ladies' room changing out of her blood-stained pants.

"Hey, it's one of the heroes of the hour. I'm Malika.... Wait, we've met before."

Delighted that she'd remembered, I held out my hand, "Paxton Gahl, we met at the river. My partner and I fished out that man-less leg." She gave an appreciative snort of a laugh.

We were still shaking hands, and I was sinking into the deep pool of Malika's eyes when Angela joined us. My partner knows me too well. Angela gave me a knowing look as I introduced them.

"Did you ever get a positive ID from that leg," I asked.

"Yep, it was the pilot. I don't imagine we'll find any more of him," Malika said.

"No, he had seventy-five percent of a burial at sea," I said stupidly. I still got a chuckle.

"Well, Paxton and Ms. Barton, I mean Angela, let me get some information for the press," she said as she removed a notebook from her hip pocket.

Afterward, on our way back to the ambulance; "Paxton and Ms. Barton, huh? I noticed she wasn't wearing a wedding band," Angela said.

"Oh," I said as if I hadn't noticed.

CHAPTER EIGHTEEN

(Anchorwoman Vicky Weber)

"Tonight's top story is a bank robbery in the Audubon Park neighborhood. Live at the scene is our own Grayson Tiller."

(Reporter Grayson Tiller)

"Yes, Vicky, according to Louisville Police spokeswoman, Sgt. Malika Kelly, an as yet, unidentified man robbed the Chambers Bank on Poplar Level Road, shooting the security guard as he entered. Here is what Sgt. Kelly had to tell us about this brazen, daylight robbery."

(Sgt. Kelly)

About 1:30 PM today, the Chambers Bank at Poplar Level Road and Hess Lane was robbed at gunpoint by a white male wearing a ski mask. The robber left the bank with an undetermined amount of cash taken from the bank tellers and was seen leaving the scene in a silver Toyota Camry traveling north. LMPD responding officers stopped a car matching the description at the intersection of Poplar Level Road and Goss Avenue. Officers ordered the driver out of the car. He complied with no resistance and was taken into custody. There were no other occupants in the suspect vehicle. The suspect's name is not being released at this time, pending possible charges."

(Reporter Grayson Tiller)

"Sgt. Kelly went on to add that both the FBI and Metro criminal investigation detectives will be looking into this robbery. Vicky, it's also important to note that an EMS crew was close at hand. We talked to Ellen Wright who was eating outside at a café next door."

(Ellen Wright)

"I heard the shot and saw this guy in a mask. Believe you me, it must have been hot in that mask. Anyway, it seems like he'd barely gotten into his car to drive off when we heard the sirens and I mean to tell you that ambulance was here lickety split. If that guard lives, it will be because of those EMS people."

(Reporter Grayson Tiller)

"Vicky, the guard, Cynthia Rodriguez is indeed alive and well at Audubon Hospital where she is listed in stable condition."

As Bloomers slowly rocked me to sleep that night, I dreamt of Malika Kelly.

CHAPTER NINETEEN

The next morning as Angela and I sat at our Audubon post, my cell lit up with a University of Louisville Hospital prefix.

"Mr. Gahl, my name is Linda with Dr. Monohan's office, I'm calling to schedule your surgery. Would Friday morning, a week from today work for you?"

She made it sound as casual as making an appointment for a haircut. "This morning would work for me," I said. I was anxious to get rid of this cancer and not crazy about waiting an entire week. "Can't Dr. Monohan do this any sooner?"

"This is the soonest the doctor and a surgical suite is available. Frankly, Mr. Gahl, this is pretty quick."

Deflated by the delay, I said, "Friday, it is."

"Dr. Monohan would like to see you on Tuesday at 8AM so we can run some labs and tell you what to expect surgically and recovery-wise," Linda said.

"I'll be there."

The volume level on my phone had crept up as these things do, and Angela had heard both sides of the conversation. After I'd stabbed the "off" image on my phone she patted my hand. "Friday will be here before you know it."

"Yeah, and then the sick leave pay I get while I'm off work will mean a pay cut because I won't be getting OT," I said. "I'm going to work every shift I can until Friday to give myself a little cushion."

"Good," said Angela, "that'll keep your mind occupied too."

So that week, after working a twelve hour shift every day with Angela, I would put in another six hours with paramedic John Cobbs. I would knock off work about 2AM and when I fell into bed, it's a safe bet that I didn't move again until the alarm woke me at 5:30 the same morning. I allowed myself a half hour to shower, shave and get to the station to meet Angela for our 6AM shift.

For the next week Angela Barton and I encountered mostly routine "hips and hearts;" broken hips and heart attacks. But in that week before my surgery there were three runs that would go into the EMT big book of history. The runs that keep this job interesting and get passed around with the principals' names changed to Smith. All these runs were for men who some EMTs refer to as 'consumers.' These are people who pretty much can't get out of their own way and require a lot of help to get through life.

Angela and I met Mr. Smith #1 on the day's last run on the Friday before my surgery. We rolled up just behind a fire truck and were waved into the backyard by a fireman on the scene. Smith had just completed his first day on a new job laying asphalt. He had gotten tar all over his new coveralls and to remove the tar, he tossed them into his parents' front-loading washer. Then he added a gallon of gasoline. Turning on the machine generated a spark and the resulting explosion blew Smith through the door behind him which, unfortunately, was closed at the time. The coveralls were a total loss. Mr. Smith would recover. Eventually.

Giving myself a light day on the Sunday before surgery, I got a shift with paramedic John Cobbs. We treated Mr. Smith #2 who accidently shot himself while cleaning his gun. In my years on the job, I'd treated many gunshot wounds, seen murders and suicides by gunshot. But I could recall only two other "while cleaning my gun" stories that I believed were just that and not a suicide or murder attempt. This call was different. This Mr. Smith shot himself with a nail gun. In his knee. John and I found him writhing on the ground in his south end Louisville back yard. Around him lay the lumber for the deck he was building. The nail gun's magazine was loaded with 2 ½" nails. The head of a nail sat like an island in a pool of blood on the knee of his blue jeans. After we converted one leg of his jeans to jean shorts, we gave him an injection for the pain. When that kicked in Smith #2 explained that he had rented the nail gun, and they were just getting acquainted when he tried to remove some dirt from the mechanism. We delivered Smith #2 to the hospital ER where an 8 by 10 print copy of his X ray still resides on the breakroom wall for all to admire.

On the day shift three days before my surgery, Angela and I met Mr. Smith #3. This Mr. Smith lived alone in an enormous pile of bricks in the exclusive east end neighborhood of Hurstbourne. He called 911 complaining of dizziness. We found him horizontal on his couch in front of a theater size plasma TV. He looked wrung out, his eyes at half mast, his speech slow. Across his lap waving the white flag of surrender was a handkerchief. It transpired that this Mr. Smith had overdosed on his erectile dysfunction medication. Smith was spent, but a lone soldier was still up for a fight. Smith #3 appeared too exhausted to be embarrassed as he explained that he'd taken one of the little blue pills with no results, so he took a second. Then a third. He'd had a boner for six hours and said he was too weak to drive himself to the ER. In a soft voice, he added, "Like before."

"Like….," Angela hesitated thinking she must have heard wrong, "before?" she said.

Smith closed his eyes. "Twice before," he said. "Just give me the shots of phenylephrine; four shots in the General there and we'll be fine."

Angela and I looked at each other with raised eyebrows. I was busy taking Mr. Smith's blood pressure, glad I was the EMT and not the paramedic in charge on this run.

"Well," Angela began, "as much as I'd like to shoot the General, Mr. Smith, we don't carry phenylephrine in our truck."

I came to Angela's rescue, "eighty-two over sixty," I said, removing the cuff.

"And," Angela continued with some relief, "your blood pressure is too low. We'll start an IV and get you to a doctor."

I know the notion that more weird things happen when there's a full moon is scientifically unfounded but every now and then I get a shift and wonder just what the hell is going on. The night before surgery, there was a full moon.

The old-fashioned way of screwing yourself up is by drinking too much and/or getting into fights, but the increasingly popular transport to this destination is via opioid OD. I think it's safe to say that every EMT on every shift treats an overdose.

John Cobbs and I were in Unit 156 and posted to a part of the city named Butchertown. This area, just east of downtown, got its name over 100 years ago because meatpackers saw it as an ideal place to locate. They could slaughter pigs and cattle and toss the remnants into Beargrass Creek as it made its way to the Ohio.

Our night went something like this:

"Unit 156, reported overdose, 729 East Washington Street."

"Unit 156, reported overdose, man down, Baxter and East Market."

"Unit 156, reported overdose, a man and a woman, North Shelby and Geiger."

"Unit 156, see the man, duct-taped to streetlight and bleeding, Baxter Avenue at Eastern Cemetery."

"Unit 156, reported overdose, woman, in the field, Barrett and Baxter Ave."

"Unit 156, reported overdose, a man and woman, North Shelby and Geiger."

"Unit 156, man down, Baxter Avenue and Broadway.

The night went fast, and we saw more patients then we might have, because all of these folks signed the form refusing to be taken to the hospital. All the overdose patients had the same symptoms and the same drug that saved their lives, Narcan. And all these people got the same message delivered from us: "If it had taken us a few minutes longer to get here, we would have lifted you with care and placed you on a stretcher. We would have covered your face with a sheet and carried you by ambulance to the basement of University Hospital. The morgue. You need to get off this shit. Here is some information where you can get help. Do it."

We called the duct-taped man Cooper Bradley because he looked a little like

Bradley Cooper. A whole roll of gray duct-tape must have been used and he was wrapped to the street light pole like a mummy. Cooper was about 5'4" with a slight build and was probably picked on all his life. We found him upside down wearing nothing but the duct tape holding him there. He was very drunk.

"Last time, I threw up all over myself, so they turned me right side......., I mean upside down this time."

"Wow, that was very thoughtful," I said while slicing through the tape with a scalpel. "But now you pissed all over yourself and into that cut on your forehead."

"How did you get that cut," asked John.

"It was an ax-dent," said Mr. Bradley. "I hit my head on the pole when they turned me over."

"Do you know when you last had a tetanus shot?" asked John, seeing dog shit near the base of the pole.

Cooper stared off into the night sky waiting for the answer that never came. John gave him a shot, and I cleaned and bandaged his wound. His thoughtful friends had left his clothes in a pile next to the dog shit.

The man and woman in the house at North Shelby and Geiger were the same couple both times we went. And both times the front door was open with no one else around. We were pretty sure God hadn't called 911, so it must have been whoever they were partying with. John Cobbs delivered the speech the first time, and I did it the second.

I went home knowing I had helped save the lives of a number of people. It had been a good day.

CHAPTER TWENTY

At the base station, I let the shift manager know I was available, grabbed one of my paramedic textbooks and read until I fell asleep. The shift supervisor, Maya Gordon, woke me an hour later by nudging my foot with a broom.

"Hey, Paxton, I've got you a ride with Charlie Altman in about 30 minutes. Ok?"

"Yeah, great," I said eyeing the broom.

"Sorry about this," she said, indicating the broom. "I couldn't remember if you were a veteran."

I was coming from a dead sleep when she hit me with this non-sequitur. All I could manage was, "Huh?"

Gordon laughed when she realized my confusion. "I almost got my head knocked off once when I woke a guy."

"No kidding. What happened?"

"This was years ago, before I took a desk job. I came to wake him because we had a shift together and I just touched his shoulder. I never saw anybody move that fast in my life. He went from peaceful snoring to on his feet, fists up in a second. He threw a punch that he stopped two inches from my face, and he was still blinking the sleep out of his eyes. Scared the hell out of me you can be sure. He spent the shift apologizing. He'd been a medic in the first Gulf War and had seen stuff that haunted him. He told me just to be on the safe side, I should wake guys around here by calling their name softly and touching their foot. The broom was my idea because I don't have a ten-foot pole."

"Whatever happened to the guy?" I asked.

"Well, the EMTs sort of ganged up on him and talked him into going to the VA. He got some help; they got him into working with his hands making things. As a hobby, he started making wooden salad tongs, you know, the kind with two pieces of wood and a hinge on one end? Then in group therapy, he met a woman who asked if she could try to market them. He found working by himself and making salad tongs a lot easier on his psyche than being an EMT. Imagine that. He sells them all over the country."

Maya paired me up with EMT Charlie Altman, and we took our first call while en route to the west end of town. Charlie was no Angela. Charlie is the kind of guy who would have the dream about being naked in front of a room full of strangers and instead of being embarrassed, he would smile and take a bow. More than a bit rough around the edges, if he had a bedside manner, he didn't bring it to work. Charlie was the piece in the EMS puzzle that just didn't fit very well. You knew the piece was supposed to go in this section over here, but it was just a little off. Medically, he knew what he was doing, but he ran into a lot of folks he dubbed "slackers," "bums" and" idiots." But his contempt wasn't confined to the general public. If we ran into an EMT who worked for Yellow Ambulance, a division of Yellow Cab, at an accident scene, Charlie would yell for all to hear, "Who the hell ordered a taxi?" And if the fire fighters we work with on a regular basis ever heard him refer to them as "hose monkeys," they might not take it kindly.

"Unit 213 meet the number 23 bus at 18th and Broadway. Man down, fallen and bleeding. Code 3."

The city bus driver told the cops Mr. Bledsoe was a "public nuisance." He had been trying to kiss women on the bus, including herself while she was driving. It wasn't clear if Nate Bledsoe had been merely asked to leave the bus at 18th Street or if a kick in the ass helped send him on his way. He landed on the bottle of rum in the paper bag he carried. It took some convincing to keep Bledsoe from trying to pull the shard of glass from his side.

"Leave that alone, let doctors pull it out," Charlie said dismissively.

It took more convincing to get Bledsoe to let loose of the neck of the broken rum bottle. He looked at it like he'd lost his best friend.

As we helped Mr. Bledsoe onto a stretcher, I got another "flash" as I decided to call them. I looked down the street to a corner liquor store where I knew a man named Pankaj Gupta had just been shot by Emmett Egan as he robbed the store.

"Hey, officer, shots fired," I yelled to the patrolman about to get into his car.

"What? Where?"

"Liquor store, there," I said pointing.

As we strapped Nate Bledsoe onto the stretcher, Charlie said, "I didn't hear any shots."

"No? I guess the cop didn't either. But you saw the guy running to his car, right?"

"Black Mustang?" said Altman.

"Could be; or maybe a navy-blue Hyundai," I said.

CHAPTER TWENTY-ONE

Charlie and I had a busy night. After delivering to the hospital an alleged "slip and fall" that had all the hallmarks of a "trip and push," we took a break in the hospital cafeteria.

I was about to sip my coffee when I got another flash. It was a shooting that startled me as if I'd suddenly materialized in the same room where one man was falling behind a green couch and the other was staring at the gun in his hand in disbelief. The hot coffee I splashed on my shirt when I jerked in surprise brought me back to the cafeteria with a start.

"Shit!"

"You're supposed to drink from the lip of the cup closest to your mouth," Charlie said laughing loudly enough to turn heads.

I gave him a disgusted look and got up as if heading for the restroom, but I hurried through the hall looking for a pay phone. There aren't many left in town, but I reasoned University Hospital would be a likely place to have them. Sure enough, I found a phone near the cafeteria but there was also a security camera on the wall opposite. That would negate an anonymous phone call, so I kept looking.

I didn't find another phone, but in the maze of corridors of the hospital, I found a cart stacked high with supplies. Keeping my head down, I pushed the cart at least fifty feet to just in front of the security camera. I called 911.

In a high voice with the worst British accent ever heard, I said, "Now see here, there's been a shooting in Smoketown. This man T.C. Johnson has shot this other man, Jeffrey Carroll. I believe the address is 2163 Clay Street. Ta Ta."

I hung up the phone and had enough time to step into the restroom and dab some water on my shirt when Charlie came running.

"Shooting. Smoketown. Let's go."

There had now been five flashes. I had to think of a way to alert the police, so I wasn't their prime suspect, or they didn't put me in a straight-jacket and haul me away to the looney bin. The solution came to me because I've watched too many police dramas on television. I went to Walgreens and bought what the TV cops call a 'burner' phone. It was just a cheap flip phone. I did an internet search to find a way to disguise my voice. The first hundred or so suggestions I located involved buying an app. My new flip phone hadn't evolved enough to know what an app was.

The voice disguise I chose came from experimentation. I covered the microphone below the keypad with a piece of paper. My voice caused the paper to vibrate enough to distort it. I called my cell phone from my burner phone and left myself messages testing different types of paper. "Hello, I'm speaking into newspaper now." "Card stock here, coming to you from card stock." The right kind of paper was the key and that turned out be a plasticized paper called vellum. I found vellum sheets separating each of the French postcards in the collection Mr. Threadgill had left behind. With a piece of tape, I made a hinge so that after punching in 911, I could flip the vellum down over the microphone.

From my job, okay and from too many TV cop shows, I knew the cell phone location could be traced, so I separated the phone from the battery until I needed it.

The last part of this puzzle was finding a way to establish credibility with the 911. I decided I could do that by giving them the same, fictitious name every time I called. After about a half an hour of searching online, I discovered ancient Romans had the answer. In Roman mythology there's a Latin name connected to fire, lightning and **flash**. The name is Vulcan.

CHAPTER TWENTY-TWO

Sitting around and laughing at the absurdity of the superhero, Vulcan Man, would have been appropriate, but I had other things on my mind — like cancer. My pre-surgery meeting with Dr. Monohan had been on Tuesday morning at the Brown Cancer Center adjacent to U of L Hospital.

"This is a particularly nasty kind of cancer you've got," Monohan said. "I will cut it out from inside your mouth and take with it a twenty-millimeter margin of tissue around the cancer as a precaution." "Dr. Eric Monohan, DMD, MD, FACS" was stitched onto his smock above the pocket. I sat with feet dangling on the examining table naked to the waist but for a paper gown that felt like it had been starched. Monohan stood in front of me with three "fellows" right behind him. I had done an on-line search and was left to wonder how he had time to operate. He was chair of the Department of Oral and Maxillofacial Surgery, had written a half dozen textbooks, had presented at conferences all over the world and he was always a teacher. As a professor at U of L, I never saw him when he didn't have at least two, and usually four fellows close at his heels. This guy was a real slacker.

"Lymph nodes are the transportation super-highway for delivering cancer cells to other parts of the body. We will remove these nodes, located right here," he said touching a spot four inches below my right cheek, "to see if cancer cells have traveled that far yet. The lab will section the nodes into more than a dozen pieces and examine each one for cancer cells. Surgery will take about three hours. You will need to stay in the hospital one night. We will send you home with two tubes coming out of the place where we cut out the lymph nodes. These are drains. The output from these drains must be measured and recorded twice a day for a week or so before I remove the tubes. You'll need someone to check on you. I understand you live alone?"

"Yes." This hadn't occurred to me. Gwen would have stepped in at this point, anticipating, knowing that I would need nursing care. But it hadn't even crossed my feeble mind.

"I'll need to make some arrangements," I said.

"After everything is healed, protocol in a case like yours calls for radiation and chemotherapy. If there are any cancer cells left, we will kill them and kill them again."

I sat there a bit stunned, I thought surgery would be the end of it.

"Hang 'em then shoot 'em," I said.

"Beg your pardon," Monohan said.

"Oh, it's something my grandmother would say about politicians caught with their hand in the till or up someone's skirt. Her blood pressure would spike, and she'd shout, 'The no-good bum; hang 'em then shoot 'em.'"

"I may have to borrow that line," he said with the first smile I'd seen.

Monohan continued, "It will be chemo once a week for five weeks. The radiation will run five days a week for five weeks."

Monohan paused to let that sink in.

"So, am I going to need to be off work all this time?"

"No. The radiation every day will only take a few minutes each time and I don't anticipate any ill effects. The chemo will take a few hours once a week. You'll get a low dose. I expect at your age and condition, you will tolerate it well."

My shrink, Dr. Newman, was in the appointments loop as promised. I had received a text the afternoon before: "Confirming your appointment at 530 South Jackson, Tuesday, 10:30AM; Text C to confirm." She offered no option if I wasn't coming. She must have known a medical avalanche was heading my way and wanted to see if I could handle it.

Newman took notes as I filled her in on the surgery, chemo, and radiation, not showing surprise about any of it. "How do you feel about this?" she asked.

"Surprised. I guess I'm still surprised. I bit down on the inside of my cheek, like, I suppose everyone has done at one time or another and find out I've bitten into a cancer. It's bizarre. But Dr. Monohan has mapped a path out of this forest, and I'll be ready."

Dr. Newman was reassuring about the surgery and then came around to asking if I'd noticed any memory problems after the ECT.

I snorted, "I don't remember who, but someone once wrote a song that said when you have nothing, you have nothing to lose."

Karen Newman smiled, "That's an old song, so I'll chalk up the lack of attribution to just a run-of-the-mill long-term memory lapse. The author was Bob Dylan. Anything else?"

I wasn't about to tell her of the flashes and that she should now call me Vulcan, but then she gave me an idea.

"At a previous visit, you mentioned a support group, is that for cancer patients or depression patients?"

"Depression, but you won't be the only one with both."

"When is that?"

"Wednesday, 8 PM, Main Library mezzanine."

"Will you be there?"

"No, that's strictly patients and former patients. I've found people are more relaxed and candid without a doctor in the house."

My boss, Brenda Trainor, is a hard ass, there's no two ways about it. She has to keep more than a hundred, young, mostly male, EMTs in line. She has the gruff and direct demeanor of a drill sergeant but one day we learned her background was Navy, not Army. On that day she silenced a large, training meeting by yelling, "quiet on the bridge." It turns out, Trainor had been a boatswain's mate in the Navy, so from that day, we called her "Boats," if she was out of earshot. To her face we called her, "Director."

The director surprised me when I reported to her office the next day before my shift. We stood on either side of her desk as she asked for details about the surgery, chemo and radiation. When I finished my brief report, she nodded as if she'd heard it all before. Then with her eyes fixed on the sheet of paper on her desk, she said, "A number of folks have come to me saying they want to help. I'm setting up a schedule for these volunteers to stop by your place to empty your drainage bowls twice a day. It'll be good training. And don't worry about the chemo and radiation; I can juggle the schedule for a few weeks."

She caught me off guard, and all I could manage was to choke out a, "thanks boss." This she swatted away like it was a pesky fly.

"Angela's waiting," she said as she turned sharply on her heel, "now get to work."

I never did find out if co-workers already working twelve-hour days had volunteered to come nurse me as she said. I think there are even odds but I am grateful either way.

CHAPTER TWENTY-THREE

The therapy group met in a small room of the main library downtown. Chairs were being formed into a circle when I arrived. Eight chairs were occupied with two extras for late arrivals. A woman who gave only the first name of Sadie started the meeting by telling us a little about herself and how her week had been since the last meeting.

"I run the Louisville Free Public Library accounting department. My office is in this building," she began.

By the time we'd gone around the circle (there were now nine of us), it was clear these background introductions had been for the benefit of the two of us who were new to the group. We had someone who worked the line at one of the Ford plants, an exec at UPS, one who worked in maintenance at the zoo, two public school teachers, a retired homemaker, and a postal worker. Six women and three men. Most in the group were taking anti-depressants, and two, besides me, had received ECTs. It was well into our hour before I asked my fellow shock jocks, the homemaker and Mr. UPS, if they'd had any unusual after-effects from the treatments.

Sean, the UPS suit, said he was a little worried about that. "If I'd been in my right mind, I would have kept a diary before the ECTs and reviewed them every day. But if I had been in my right mind, I don't suppose I'd needed shock treatments." He'd had ten treatments. Emily, a woman in her seventies who described herself as a homemaker, had her ECTs twenty years before and came to the group for "maintenance." She reported no side effects, just a vast improvement in her mental health.

Emily said, "What about you, any after-effects?"

I looked at the faces around the room and balked at disclosure, "Just the seeing through walls bit, but that's fading a little every day."

Sadie thought that a laugh was a good way to end the session, so we called it a night.

CHAPTER TWENTY-FOUR

At Friday around noon, I awoke in the recovery room after a dream about an exciting Cincinnati Reds vs. the Chicago Cubs game where Malika Kelly and I are caught on the kissing cam in front of a packed stadium. She was on my lap, my hand had disappeared inside her blouse, and the caption below our lip-locked image on the big screen in left field read, "Get A Room Already." As I opened my eyes, I could hear two people who seemed to be talking about my dream. My eyes opened on the TV showing a baseball game. The sound was low. Then the fog cleared, and I realized my brother Phillip was talking baseball with Cliff. I lay still for a minute until I was sure I had separated the dream from the conversation.

"There he is," Phillip said when he noticed I was coming around. With my eyes half open, I groggily looked from one to the other on opposite sides of the bed. They both wore shit-eating grins. I took this as a sign that despite the golf ball in my cheek, the surgery had gone well. Finally, Phillip said, "Cliff tells me Louisville has a zombie walk this week."

Talk about your non-sequitur, I answered a tentative, "Yeah?"

With Crunchy nodding like an idiot, Phillip said, "You're gonna win."

He pulled out his cell phone and took my picture. The right side of my face was swollen, the gauze stuffed inside my cheek must have helped, and two clear tubes came out of my neck below my chin. The tubes directed a slow flow of dark red ooze into two bulbous rubber pouches pinned to my gown.

"First prize for most realism in a zombie costume goes to Paxton Gahl," declared Crunchy as he raised his arms in the air like a referee signaling a touchdown. Thinking the anesthetic was playing games with my head, I closed my eyes and went back to sleep.

The next thing I knew, Doctor Monohan swept in trailing his entourage. There was a smile on his face. Without preamble he began.

"All went well. The lab report on cancer cells in the lymph nodes was negative. How do you feel?"

"Okay." And I threw in a thumbs-up in case he hadn't understood my gauze impaired mumble.

Monohan pulled out the gauze and had a look around. Satisfied with what he saw, each of the fellows donned gloves and asked if they could have a look.

In the morning, Dr. Monohan released me from the hospital and Phillip drove me home to Bloomers, where he had stayed overnight.

"I don't know how you can sleep in this thing. As soon as I got used to the rockin' side to side, it would rock front to back."

"Well, I had an advantage. I was drunk when I was getting used to it. Now, I don't even notice. Stay a few days, and you'll be sleeping like a baby."

"No can do, bro. The girls are driving Amanda batty. I have to get back to Cincy this afternoon."

Twelve years before, Phillip and Amanda had married. They graduated from high school in June and Amanda gave birth to twin girls that winter. The first one down the chute was named Summer, she was followed by, what else, Autumn. These things happen when teenagers have children.

"Let me show you what we have for your dining pleasure," Phillip said as he bowed and directed me to the galley. The word was out that I could eat nothing but soft foods for a week. The cupboard was full of soups, applesauce, and micro-wave oatmeal. From the Blue Dick at one end of the dock, Richard Bush had delivered a dozen packages of ready-to-eat puddings and from the other end of the dock, the Shepards had made a batch of home-made cream of chicken soup. I was a lucky man.

CHAPTER TWENTY-FIVE

"9-1-1, what's your emergency?"

"A woman has fallen and hit her head, she's unconscious and bleeding. In the Zachary Taylor Cemetery on Brownsboro Road. Turn left at the entrance, Section A. This is Vulcan."

I hit the 'off' button and removed the battery as if it were on fire in my hands. This time I wasn't sure if this had been a flash, or a dream. I'd been dozing in my Lazy-Boy recliner waiting for "60 Minutes" to start when eighty-year-old Alice Satterfield had woken me up by tripping at the grave of her brother, Sergeant John Squires. I'd never been in the Zachary Taylor Cemetery; I'd never heard of Sergeant Squires and didn't know if there was a Section A.

But an on-line search confirmed all the above. Squires was described as a brave soldier who had died in Padiglione, Italy on May 23, 1944 about a year before the Germans surrendered in Europe to end the war there. Sergeant Squires earned the Medal of Honor, posthumously.

Angela arrived wearing her civvies, carrying a padded nylon bag. She was being followed. In a voice dripping with tease and lechery, she said "Pax, this is my friend Tessa." Tessa had about her a shyness that was incongruous for someone wearing a snow-white halter top and low-rise red shorts that began a hand width below her navel. She was a couple of inches taller than Angela, who was herself 5'9", and anorexic enough to be a model.

When Angela came into the room closer to me, she didn't waste that silky smooth, calming voice on me.

"Holy crap, Pax, you look like you've been drug through a knot-hole sideways."

"It's good to see you too, Ange," I said standing up. "I've been assured I will knock 'em dead at the zombie walk next week.

"Tessa, welcome to Bloomers. I can give you both a full tour and you won't have to leave the spot where you're standing. Bedroom, bathroom, living room, kitchen," I said pointing out each.

Angela gave me a beady-eyed look, "I've been here twice before Pax. Of course, you were shit-faced both times."

"Ah, sorry," I said.

She let me off the hook with, "Maybe it was the ECT. They said you might have a short-term memory problem."

"Yeah," I said doubtfully, "maybe that's it."

Angela started to say something, but I plunged on, "So, can I offer some horror makeup tips?"

"No, I have fixed you dinner," Angela announced. "But first," she said as she snapped on rubber gloves, "I believe it's time to drain some ooze."

CHAPTER TWENTY-SIX

I'd had lots of company and had been out walking on the docks, but the Knights of Columbus area wasn't conducive to long strolls. I couldn't drive with the tubes dangling from my neck and cabin fever was setting in when Crunchy called. He offered to come by with the boys and take me out for a milkshake. I was ready.

Cliff drove Liam, Noah, and me east on River Road toward the prosperous community of Prospect. Cliff knows the area well because if people have trouble with their million-dollar homes settling awkwardly or want to add a 2,000-square foot deck, he is liable to get a call. To entertain the boys as he drove, Cliff lowered his voice and became a TV narrator. "Now we will go back in time, to the beginning of the last century. This road we are on was being built with gravel over a dirt path carved into the woods by deer and other wild animals. The house we are going to was being built for a young couple who already had four of the eight children they would eventually have. Today, one of the grandchildren lives with her family upstairs in the house and operates a café on the ground floor." Then I got a flash.

"Oh hell-ck," I stumbled, remembering the boys. "I've got to take a leak, Cliff. Just pull over here and I'll go behind a tree."

"We're almost…," he started.

"Sorry, but it's got to be now please." I was sure he'd credit the urgency to my recent surgery. We were in an exclusive part of the county where houses are enormous and isolated, buffered by hundreds of acres of woody, rolling landscape.

Cliff gave me a quick look but pulled over without another word. I went farther into the woods than modesty required.

"9-1-1, what's your emergency?"

"Single car crash, on Rose Island Road, 100 yards north of Jerry Tucker Way. The car left the road at high speed, deep into the woods. Serious injury. This is Vulcan." I flipped the phone shut and popped the battery as I walked back to the car.

What I hadn't told the 911 operator was that the BMW Z4 was driven by a sixteen-year-old girl whose vision was curtained by tears. I learned later she'd had a fight with her boyfriend. Any parent who would give a sixteen-year-old a ton and a half of sportscar, capable of 155mph, should be arrested for negligence. Maybe it wasn't as bad as giving a four-year-old a torch in a match factory, but it was close.

Not knowing the area or where Cliff was taking us beforehand, it wasn't until he made a turn and I saw the street sign, Rose Island Road, that I realized we were coming up to the scene of the accident. It was too early for police cars or EMS ambulances, and I didn't hear any sirens.

"Stop," I yelled. Cliff had been looking to his left, out over the fields, and I'm sure the boys were looking to the right where there was a privately-owned petting zoo called Henry's Ark.

No doubt I about gave Cliff a heart attack. He slammed his foot on the brake and we skidded to a stop.

"What. What is it? Did I hit something?"

"No, a car's run off the road."

Cliff looked for a second, "Where, I don't see it."

"I saw it from back there, it's behind those trees. Call 9-1-1." As soon as I got out of the car, I smelled gasoline. "Tell them to send the fire department too."

I ran into the woods, my right arm shielding my tubes from the claws of the brush. Cliff made the call, parked his car, and shouted instructions at the boys giving them responsibility to wave down EMS and Fire.

The fact is that I hadn't seen the car from the roadway but there were tire tracks off the road and a five-foot Douglas fir which may have made a great Christmas tree in a few months, was now pulp. I was sure the car was there.

You don't remove an unconscious person from a wrecked car without proper training and precautions, but the car was on fire. The nose of the late model Z4 was molded around a tree trunk. Flames came from under the hood, but the gas tank was in the back.

I'm a bit embarrassed about the rest of the story, so I'll just submit the newspaper account.

> The Louisville Courier
>
> Louisville, Kentucky
>
> *There was a serious injury accident yesterday afternoon from a single car crash in far-eastern Jefferson County. The accident was reported at 2:05 PM on Rose Island Road near the popular petting zoo, Henry's Ark. Sixteen-year-old Kelsey Spaar was northbound when the sports car she was driving failed to make the turn. Spaar was taken by air ambulance to the trauma center at University Hospital. Her condition is listed as serious but stable. Her injuries include major head, chest, and neck trauma. There were no witnesses to the accident, but Cliff Reilly, out for a drive with a friend and his girlfriend's sons, said there is a clear hero.*
>
> *"My friend, Pax, is recovering from oral surgery for cancer and he's on a soft foods diet, so the boys and I thought we'd take him out for a milkshake. I don't know how he saw that car buried in those bushes. But Pax is an EMT, and he was out of my car in a flash. By the time I got there, he was carrying the girl to safety. The car was completely engulfed in flames. I hope she pulls through, and if she does, it will be because of Paxton Gahl."*
>
> *Gahl was treated at the scene by fellow EMTs for lacerations and a minor burn on his leg.*

Next to the story was a color photo taken by one of the folks who'd come running from the petting zoo. It could have been a movie poster for "Vulcan Zombie" showing Kelsey Spaar cradled in my arms, limp as a dishrag, the frame caught me with both feet off the ground, my pants leg torn (actually burned) away, blood-red drainage tubes coming out of my neck, and a fire-ball behind me because the gas tank had just exploded. It was all too much.

Word travels fast in the EMS, fire and police community and by the time Cliff got me back to Bloomers, the well-wishers had started to arrive with atta-boys and even some gifts. Around sunset, having just watched the rescue story on the evening news, I heard a familiar voice just outside my open cabin door. Malika Kelly asked permission to come aboard.

CHAPTER TWENTY-SEVEN

Sgt. Malika Kelly stopped by to congratulate me on my off-duty rescue. I almost didn't recognize her. Her brown hair fell below her shoulders. On duty, her hair was braided and pinned close to her head. Off-duty, Malika looked very different than Sgt. Kelly. She wore khaki shorts and a light green sleeveless shirt. Her police uniform had been hiding arms that were sculpted with subtlety. Her long, tan legs looked ready for a spur of the moment half marathon. And finally, there were those beautiful hazel eyes, two of them.

Malika hadn't come empty handed when she'd visited me aboard Bloomers. She came bearing a gift of Mott's Applesauce. It was clear she'd seen the newspaper story and had been filled in about my recent cancer surgery and soft food diet. I was, of course, excited to see her and worked hard to make a good impression.

"My parents had a cruiser about this size when I was young," she said as she looked around. "It was strictly a weekend thing. I don't think we ever spent the night on board. And you live here," she said, incredulously.

Wanting to show off my vocabulary, I said, "Yep."

"They denied it, but I think they sold the boat to help pay my tuition at Ohio University."

"Go Buckeyes!" I said with brilliance.

"Bobcats," she corrected, "Go Bobcats, Buckeyes are Ohio State," she said. "OU has a police academy."

"Ah, I see. Are your parents still.... um, with us?" I fumbled.

"Yes. In Florida. Yours?"

"St. Louis. I mean, Louisville but in St. Louis Cemetery. I mean, they both passed away years ago." I felt like I was dancing with a girl for the first time. "Twelve years ago, within six months of each other."

"Oh, I'm sorry." Malika had taken me up on the offer of a glass of iced tea when she walked in the door and at the rate I was going, she'd be looking for the nearest exit within minutes.

But I floundered on, "I'm not ready to claim bad genes yet since they were both heavy smokers right up till the end. For dad, it was his heart and mother her lungs. But enough about this morbid subject."

"Yeah, it's not like we don't see enough death in our business. So," she said as she cast about for a change of subject. Her eyes landed on a framed 'bloomers' postcard of a half-naked woman. She did not sigh so much as deflate just a little and I instantly regretted framing the card.

"It came with the boat," I said lamely, "along with the name, which I just bought this summer. The boat that is, not the name. Although, I guess I bought the name too. Post-divorce impulse purchase." Hastily I added, "I need to come up with a new name."

At that, Malika perked up a bit. "Well, that could be fun."

"Fun? No, not so far," I said. "If you think of one, I'd like to hear it."

"I'll work on that."

"Excellent."

She took a tentative sip of her iced tea and sat down on the edge of a chair. Her posture relaxed just a little, but her feet, clad in white running shoes with purple trim, were still poised as if in starting blocks and aimed toward the door. I was making dazzling progress.

"Didn't I read that your leg was burned when you rescued Kelsey Spaar?" she said looking for evidence.

"They exaggerated a little, I mainly singed a lot of the hair off my right leg. My EMT buddies smothered it in petroleum jelly." Looking down, I added, "which by now I've probably smeared all over this couch."

"Knock, Knock," came a female voice from the gangway, "I'm here for your evening blood-letting."

It was my boss, Brenda. And just as I was on the verge of sweeping Malika off her feet with my wit and charm.

No introductions were necessary, and the two women greeted each other by their first names and began exchanging pleasantries. They ignored me. Then Malika said, "I need to be going."

My, "No, wait," was followed by a lengthy pause as I tried to figure out why she should wait. Finally, the dawn rose among the little gray cells, "You owe me a boat name."

Malika looked into my eyes for several beats and reached a decision.

"Give me your phone number," she said as she pulled her own phone out of her hip pocket. "I need to think about it."

I gave myself a mental high five. I had her phone number. Ok, so I only had it if she actually called me first. Of course, she would call.

CHAPTER TWENTY-EIGHT

Dr. Monohan removed my drainage tubes the following Friday morning and cleared me to work. Chemo and radiation would begin in about a month. It was the start of a beautiful Labor Day weekend and Brenda Trainor put out the call for all hands on-deck. I reported for duty at noon.

Taped to the locker room wall of EMS HQ, was a poster size version of my newspaper photo. The word "Hero" was added below. Good-natured razzing and high fives were going to continue for a while. My partner Angela was standing by our truck when I emerged from the locker room. She bowed and opened the passenger door as I approached, "Your carriage, sir."

"I just want to be treated like one of you, the little people," I pleaded.

I had seven flashes over the holiday weekend. Vulcan only made five calls because two of those flashes were injury accidents on busy streets, and since everybody has a cell phone, I knew there would be someone to call them in. For the other five flashes I had to find excuses to get away from Angela in order to call 911. Once, I slipped around to the other side of the truck at the scene of a minor accident and three times I said I had an urgent need for a bathroom. One flash came as Angela was getting us each a cup-a-joe at Day's Coffee in the Highlands. Add those fake bathroom breaks to the regular, real ones and Angela was getting concerned. I thought the concern was about my bladder. I was wrong.

Returning at 5AM on Monday of the Labor Day weekend, the big boss, Brenda Trainor met our truck. We stepped down from the ambulance, and she handed us each a small container.

"I need a urine sample before you go home," she said smiling. "Bring it to the office, you know the routine."

Random drug tests were normal; they'd been doing them since I started work for Louisville EMS. But this was different. This test was called after a shift and not before. I looked to Angela and saw the glisten of a tear in her eye before she turned her head away from me. All at once, I saw the whole picture through her eyes. Her partner went from a drinking problem to sneaking off frequently during the shift for, what? Alcohol would have been obvious. Angela must think I'm doing pain killers when I go to call in a flash. She must have called Brenda when on her own bathroom break to pass on her suspicions. My partner and friend thought I was going down. I had to find some way to tell Angela about the flashes.

CHAPTER TWENTY-NINE

On busy holiday weekends, EMS work shifts get out of whack, and Angela and I were scheduled to be back on duty Monday night at 10PM. At 7 that evening, I sent her a text. "How about dinner. 8? at D. Nalley?"

I had spent the previous hour making a study of the flashes I'd already had. I made a chart of where I was when I'd gotten a flash, and where the event was that had triggered the flash. I saw the obvious; the events were always near wherever in the city I happened to be, usually within a few blocks. If that was the case, then dinner at D. Nalley's Restaurant in a densely populated location might provide the trigger for another flash. The flashes, so far, had all been the routine things we cover on the job as EMTs. So Old Louisville, as it's known, was a good place for my plan. A great place to be if you're looking for that kind of action.

Angela's text read, "See u then."

Dinner was awkward. When you spend as much time together as we did, small talk over dinner can be a little forced. When the food arrived, we were both pleased to have something to keep our mouths busy. Angela teased me with a big juicy burger while I, still on soft, thin food because I couldn't open my mouth all the way, had to settle for small bites of a grilled cheese sandwich.

"So, how's Tessa?" I asked between nibbles.

"Oh, that's not going anywhere. But it will be fun for a while. She's a few bricks short of a load."

After more silence, I took a leap.

"You don't have to worry about my drug test. I'm clean."

"Oh, thank god," she said putting down her burger and resting her fingers on her temples. "You've been acting weird and I didn't know..."

"Wait, wait, just let me tell you what's going on first and keep in mind that the drug test I had this morning will prove I'm clean, despite what you're about to hear."

I had her full attention. I took a sip of coffee and continued, "Ever since the ECT, I've been getting what I call flashes. Suddenly, in my mind, I have a clear picture of an accident or injury or some act of violence. In real time. The kind of things you and I see all day long."

I looked at Angela to get a clue as to how she was taking this, but that face I knew so well was giving nothing away.

"The very first one of these flashes happened when Crunchy was driving me home from the hospital...."

In mid-sentence, what I'd been hoping for, another flash. My smile was probably maniacal. I held up a finger and said, "Ah perfect, arson." I pulled out my burner phone from one pocket, my wallet and the phones' battery from another. "We have to go. Eat up."

After I assembled and powered up the phone, I laid it on the table so that Angela could see me fold back the vellum and punch in three numbers.

"9-1-1, what's your emergency?"

I looked right into Angela's wide open, big brown eyes and said, "Arson, 926 Hepburn Avenue, basement, rear entrance, courtesy of a Jack Ewing. His grandmother is an invalid on the second floor, unconscious. She's alone in the house. This is Vulcan." I pulled the battery from the phone, threw down too much money for dinner and said, "Let's go, you'll need to see this."

Angela sat frozen, her mouth agape, so I gently reached down to take her elbow and help her up. I kept talking, telling her about the other flashes as I led her to the car. We were half-way to the Hepburn address when I got to the story of the old lady at Zachary Taylor Cemetery.

She perked up, excited, "I made that run. I made that run. We couldn't figure out who would leave an old lady alone and unconscious in a cemetery."

"Was she alright?"

"Yeah. Lost a lot of blood; you know head wounds."

"Banged her head on her brother's tombstone when she tripped," I said.

I parked a half block away from the Hepburn address in a neighborhood known as The Original Highlands. Construction on houses in the neighborhood had begun shortly after the Civil War. Most of the houses on the street are three-story, wood-framed and a painting contractor's wet dream. Each of these homes is painted three or more colors and they're known collectively as the "painted ladies." Two-thirds of the houses had been kept up and are beauties. Number 926 — not so much. This one was purple with yellow shutters.

"Maybe our fire-bug is aesthetically sensitive," said Angela.

The closest fire department was only a few blocks away, and the firefighters were hard at it when we arrived. No flames were visible, but there was plenty of smoke pouring from first floor windows. Out the front door an old woman in a night dress came supported by a firefighter on each arm.

Angela spotted an arson investigator who'd taught a class she'd taken. "Patricia, err, Major Kaplan," she shouted as she ran her hands over her hair.

"Hey, Angela, how are you." Patricia Kaplan had a big smile on her face and a smoke detector held by the fingertips of both gloved hands.

"I was in the neighborhood. I go on duty in a while and I guess I can't help but chase firetrucks. Faulty smoke detector?" she asked.

Kaplan was so lost looking into Angela's eyes, she had to look down at what she was holding. Then Kaplan looked over at me.

"Oh," Angela said, "I'm sorry, Major Kaplan, this is my partner, my EMT partner, Paxton Gahl."

"Pleased to meet you Major."

"You can both call me Patricia. Hey, you're the zombie EMT," she said with a smile.

"Yes, but you can call me Pax."

"Somebody made a poster of that newspaper photo of you and we have it taped to a mirror at the station."

Angela said, "Yeah, we did that at our station too."

"Probably not like ours though. Consider it as professional jealousy, but we cut your head out and taped the rest to a mirror. Presto, we're all heroes."

We all enjoyed a good laugh and then Kaplan leaned in toward Angela like I wasn't there and said, "We got an anonymous call about this fire being an arson. The old lady was knocked on the head. I found the smoke detector as you see it, with the battery compartment slid out so the battery was disconnected. I'm betting whoever opened it didn't bother to worry about fingerprints because they figured the whole unit would have burned up."

"Oh, I'd love to hear what you find out. Could you give me a call, I'd love to hear more about this?" The second time she used the word 'love' must have been in case Kaplan missed it the first time.

Angela reached into her shirt pocket and pulled out a business card. But Patricia Kaplan wasn't going to let loose of that smoke detector.

"Put it in my pocket," Kaplan said as she thrust her right breast in Angela's direction. Angela used both hands for this operation, one to open the pocket, the other to insert the card. Both women giggled. I had to avert my eyes and feign interest in the firefighters who were starting to put away equipment.

As soon as we were out of earshot, I mocked in a falsetto, "I'd love to hear more about this."

CHAPTER THIRTY

The text message from a number I didn't know came at 1AM. I smiled and held the phone for Angela to see.

She read, "Da Boat," and said, "What's that?"

I spoke into our truck's microphone without pressing the 'talk' button. "Houston, we have contact."

"Oh, it's Malika. Well, it took her long enough." I had filled Angela in on the boat name conversation with Malika Kelly the week before. And had about given up hope of hearing from her.

I texted back, "Good, but looking for great. A boat's expensive, what about An Arm & A Leg?"

In a few minutes, came the reply, "Hmmm, going to sleep on it. 'Night."

Suddenly, Angela sat up straighter in the driver's seat. "But, that's it. You can tell Kelly about Vulcan."

There had been a downpour for most of the night and we'd had only two runs, an OD and a non-injury accident. So, we'd been kicking around ideas for turning me into the authorities. I had two requirements: that I not be considered a suspect of any of the crimes I had reported and that I not be carted off to the funny farm. Already, my task had become easier now that Angela knew. I had made two calls as Vulcan that night, minutes apart. The first was a drug overdose and Angela had us underway as I dialed 911. We were running Code 3 when I got the second flash and had to switch off the siren and report that Sheila McMorrow, who had at least fifty pounds on her husband Don, had just cracked his head with a cast-iron frying pan.

"I guess the police information officer would be in the loop about these 9-1-1 calls," I said.

Angela ignored me as she searched the police website for information about anonymous calls or the name Vulcan.

"Nothin'," she said when she was finished.

"Ok, let's keep an eye out for her and look for an opportunity to tell her."

As I lay down to go to bed at nine in the morning, my phone chirped with a text.

I read, "Buckeye."

I replied, "Bobcat."

Angela and I had the rest of Tuesday off work until Wednesday morning at 6AM as we transitioned back to our regular day shifts. I woke around 3PM and checked my phone to find a text from Sgt. Kelly. "S.S. Minnow?"

I replied, "Band-Aid?"

Wednesday, we were posted to the south end of town and parked our truck near Iroquois Amphitheater. There is a large immigrant community concentrated in this part of town. Unlike the rest of the country, Louisville has almost the same number of immigrants from Asian countries as we do from the Caribbean and Latin American countries. Not all of them are in the U.S. legally.

At 11:15AM, I got a flash that Isabella Fernandez was getting the hell beat out of her by Donald Jones, just blocks away from where we were parked. I assembled my burner phone and Angela threw the ambulance in gear. Then I stopped and pulled the battery back out.

"What if Fernandez is illegal," I said. "I call this in, and she could get deported."

"The cops don't report illegals to immigration. Make the call," said Angela.

"You sure?"

"90%," she said.

I made the call. The address was a small brick house that had seen better days. The one window on the front of the house was missing a shutter, a window screen lay on the ground below the window. The gravel drive was empty. A car was parked in the front yard.

As Angela skidded to a stop, I jumped out of the truck.

"Wait for the cops," she shouted as I ran for the front door.

I had barely hung up the phone, the cops could be another ten minutes. I wasn't waiting.

Angela hit the siren again, hoping, I guess to scare Don Jones into thinking the cavalry had arrived. My fist hit the door once as Jones opened it. He reached down to zip up his pants.

"Step out Jones," I commanded, "where is she?"

Jones' 5'5" height was a match for his girth. He stood open mouthed, but he didn't answer. We could hear a siren approaching. Angela had grabbed the only weapon she could find and came on the run swinging a Maglite. She had seen him zip his fly.

"Did you rape her you piece of shit," she screamed down into his face. Jones could only look from one to the other of us and say, "How?"

Angela had burst from her 5'9" frame like park rangers tell you to do when confronting a bear on the trail. She was larger than life. Jones looked like a guy who'd pulled the pin from the grenade before finding it was glued to his hand. I slammed a shoulder into him to clear the doorway. The house only had four small rooms, hardly bigger than my boat. I reached the bedroom in time to see through the open window, into the backyard, Isabella Fernandez running from the house. She was pulling her torn blouse around her and didn't stop at my offers to help. She probably didn't know who to trust.

While one of the LMPD officers questioned Jones, the other, named Roberto Sanchez according to the shiny brass name tag on his uniform, explained to Angela and me that he was sympathetic, but they had no reason to hold Jones. He said that Isabella probably ran because she was illegal.

"We have orders to turn suspected illegal aliens over to ICE," the Immigration and Customs Enforcement agency, he said.

"So, these people are prey to sleaze bags like this," Angela said pointing to

Jones. "And they can't call you guys for help for fear they would be deported."

"It's often worse than that," Sanchez said, "because some of these immigrants are coming from places where the cops are corrupt. They do not trust the police."

Angela took a long look at Jones and then walked over to where he leaned against the police car.

"Listen hear, shit-for-brains, we know who you are and where you live. We're watching you. You pull any of this shit again and we'll know about it just like we knew this time. I will come back here with a microscope and personally cut off your tiny dick and shove it down your throat. Do you understand?" Angela had punctuated each sentence by spiking a finger into his chest.

Looking from one patrolman to the other, he said, "Hey she threatened me just then. That was a threat. You have to arrest her for threatening my person."

Sanchez looked over at his partner who shrugged his shoulders and said, "I didn't hear anything."

Sanchez looked at Jones and said, "I need my hearing checked." They gave a nod in our direction and headed to their police cars. We walked to the ambulance.

Jones said, "Hey wait, how did you know my name. How did you know her name?"

We kept walking.

CHAPTER THIRTY-ONE

Text from Malika: "Sail La Vie."
Text from Pax: "Sailabration."

It was time for me to ask Malika out on a date. Radiation and chemotherapy were scheduled in a couple of weeks and the physical after-effects of those treatments were not expected to be bad, but there were no guarantees. Angela and Cliff were nudging me along and both had suggested double dating. I had thought my dating days had ended nine years before when I'd gotten married. I was out of practice and I was never good at it when I was in practice.

Texting had become our method of communication, so I decided to try that way. "Dinner Friday?"

Malika's reply came quickly. "? For a boat name?"

Texts are like emails; you can't tell if someone is being coy. "Sorry, I was trying to ask you out on a date," I texted back.

This time the reply was slow in coming. I checked my bars. I went up on the top deck hoping for better reception. I sank into a deck chair. I sank deeper with each minute that passed.

Finally, the reply. "Thanks, but I'm seeing someone. I have a date."

I answered with, "Titanic."

CHAPTER THIRTY-TWO

By the time Friday night rolled around, I'd looked at Malika's last message enough times that I'd managed to find a ray of hope. She did words for a living; they were important to her. If her text had stopped at "Thanks, but I'm seeing someone," that would have said to me, "Go away, leave me alone." But she had added, "I have a date." So maybe if she hadn't had a date, she may have gone out with me, even though she was seeing someone. Ok, I was reaching, I would have preferred just the last sentence of that text, "I have a date," but I could work with what I got.

But I had no date and Cliff was tied up with his new family. Angela didn't want to work over-time and I didn't want to partner with someone else and have to sneak around whenever I got a flash. Hanging out on Bloomers seemed like a bad idea. It was a beautiful weekend and all the river-rats would be out partying on their boats. Beer would be flowing. Temptation would be great. I decided to take in a Bats game.

Louisville has a minor league, Triple A baseball team, an affiliate to the Cincinnati Reds called the Louisville Bats. The name being a homage to the famous baseball bat manufacturer of the Louisville Slugger, just down Main Street from Slugger Field where the Bats play. I knew there would be the call of "Cold beer here, get your cold beer here," but at $5 a cup plus tip, it was a temptation I thought I could withstand. It was to be a busy night.

I was still following doctor's orders and eating only soft foods. The Slugger Field menu had only one item that met the requirement and I was settled in down the first base line with a bowl of chili balanced on my knee, when I got a flash. The flash came from across the river in Jeffersonville, Indiana, a distance of over a mile. I put the bowl of chili under my seat and draped my napkin over it. I begged pardon of my neighbors for needing to shuffle down the row again, explaining that I needed a cold beverage for the hot chili. Walking through the crowd that always mills about among the vendors, I assembled my burner phone and dialed.

"9-1-1, what's your emergency?"

"This is Vulcan. An old man, named Abe Padgett was just mugged behind the building at the corner of West Market and Court Street in Jeffersonville. Broken jaw, I think. The mugger was Graham Levy and he is on a bicycle, east bound on Market."

I started to hang up and then heard, "Wait, did you say Gam."

I knew the problem was the vellum. "Graham, G-R-A-H-A-M; Levy, L-E-V-Y."

As I hung up the phone, I heard the crack of a bat and looked up to see a foul ball coming my way into the stands. There was a mad scramble as three teenage boys pushed and shoved anyone in their path to get to the ball. It bounced off a seat toward me. The biggest boy lunged for the ball and I deflected it to a kid of about seven wearing a baseball glove, ball cap on backwards standing in the aisle. The kid fielded the ball neatly in his glove using both hands as he had been taught. One of the teenagers jumped toward the kid, and the boy's mother in her Army Ranger camos squared off behind her son. The teenager stopped like he'd hit a wall. Fans nearby applauded the boy for his brilliant catch, and they were joined seconds later by the whole stadium as his image appeared on the hi-def, three-story video screen in center field.

Back at my seat, I managed to slurp down my chili while it was still warm. As I settled back to watch a game that the Bats were now losing 2-1 to the Carolina Clippers, I got another flash. There was a single car, injury accident on the I-64 overpass, about a ¼ mile away. I wasn't going to call this in because there probably were plenty of motorists about to do that, but from reflex, I reached into my pocket. In all the excitement over the foul ball, I'd forgotten to remove the battery. I took a look around and saw police officers, not casually hanging about on their beat, but actively scanning the crowd, cell phones to their ears. The police had tracked my phone signal to the stadium. If I'd been out on the street, they would have nailed me, but everybody in the place had a cell phone. I was just another tree in the forest. The burner phone rang. I reached into my pocket and wrapped my hand around the phone in a death grip to smother the ringing.

A Bats player hit a long drive into right field, and I screamed my approval and then complained loudly when the ball was caught on the warning track. Finally, the phone stopped ringing and I pulled it out of my pocket. I kept my eyes fixed on the ball field, not wanting to be seen answering or handling a phone. Without looking down, I counted on the mechanics of memory to help me remove the battery. From early experiments, I knew the phone vibrated, a second before it rang. I felt that vibration just as I flipped the battery out with a fingernail.

I made myself sit there until the end of the inning, then flowed into the crowd which was heading for a bathroom or refreshments. I avoided the eyes of the LMPD officers and was near my exit when I felt a firm tap on my shoulder. I turned to a smiling policeman who said, "Hey, aren't you the EMT hero?"

"Hey, hi. I don't know about that. Right place, right time is all."

"No, no, don't under-rate what you did. You're a hero man, I just wanted to shake your hand."

I almost said it was already shaking, but I wiped a sweaty palm on my pants leg, and shook his hand. "Thanks."

I almost made it to my car when I got another flash. I dialed those three digits and instead of, "9-1-1, what's your emergency," the male voice said, "You again, now what."

I shouldn't have been surprised but was. After a moment I said, "A murder or at least a death. Martin Flint has just sent his wife, Paula to the great beyond by entertaining her with erotic asphyxiation." I had the operator's attention now. Paula Flint was the wealthy scion of a Kentucky bourbon distillery magnate. Pampered her whole life by parents, nannies and servants, she had been putting dinner on the tables of tabloid reporters since she was 17. Sex videos, drug arrests, and a spectacular DUI in the Hamptons, where she totaled her Lamborghini. The $250,000, burnt orange beauty she was driving "left the road at a high rate of speed and became air-borne" according to news reports. The wedged shaped nose of the car sliced into the side of a new sailboat sitting on its trailer. The boat was to be a birthday gift from Elon Musk to his wife and he had it delivered the next morning with the car still impaled.

"Martin Flint turned the gas on the stove thinking to make it look like an accident. He's headed to Bowman Field Airport. Paula Flint is in their condo on Billy Goat Strut." I hung up without my usual sign-off and pulled the battery.

Billy Goat Strut and Nanny Goat Strut are alleys that got their names because European immigrants used to enjoy racing goats in the area in the early 1900's. The old industrial buildings in the neighborhood have been converted to very pricey condos. The Flints' place was a short distance from Slugger Field, so I decided to walk. Media interest would be high in a case like this and Malika Kelly was sure to be at the scene. I took perverse pleasure in the knowledge that her date would be interrupted.

It was time to introduce Malika to Vulcan.

CHAPTER THIRTY-THREE

Sgt. Malika Kelly had earned the respect of the press because she believes the public has a right to know what is going on in their city. She is aware of every reporter's deadline; she understands their need to ask questions for which they already know the answer and the need to be able to quote someone in authority. She knows which questions she can answer and which questions she must not. Sgt. Kelly shows the reporters respect and they returned the favor. She took their calls anytime, day or night. She treats the rookie reporter the same as the veteran and is known to help the rookies ask the right question.

So, on the night of Paula Flint's death, when Sgt. Kelly asked that TV cameras only film her from the waist up and asked all the media to not report on her wardrobe, they did as she asked. The reason for the request was that Kelly and her date had been at a formal fund-raiser in support of a scholarship fund for children of police officers who died in the line of duty. Malika came directly from the event wearing a sleeveless, floor length, emerald green gown. Her shoulder length brown hair was freed from its on-duty restraints. I was convinced evening wear was appropriate for the death of Paula Flint, but I could see where others would disagree.

Like all officers, Malika had a take-home car. In her case, it was a tricked-out, unmarked black van with a couple of captain's chairs in the back, carpeted floor and walls, two TV monitors and plenty of lighting. She buttoned on a uniform blouse over her dress, traded her high heels for black Pumas and corralled her flowing locks. On this night she would conduct press briefings from inside the van and out of the sight of freelancers with cell-phone cameras.

I scanned the crowd, drawn by the accumulation of police cars, an EMS ambulance and a firetruck which was sent to cut off the flow of natural gas and clear the odor from the building. I saw no man in formal attire. Malika was there, but not her date.

A uniformed patrol officer stood by the side of the van and ushered in TV news crews, radio and print journalists one at a time. When the last reporter stepped out of the van, I approached the officer.

"Paxton Gahl from The Bugle," I said mentioning the name of an upscale, mostly east-end weekly magazine that carried a high percentage of glossy photographs. Paula Flint's photo would have been in The Bugle many times because she patronized and donated to the arts. The Derby issue would have had several photos of the Flints as they flitted from one Derby party to the next. Readers of The Bugle would have to learn of Paula's tabloid escapades elsewhere, because they wouldn't see them mentioned in that publication. Her obit would appear in The Bugle, I was sure, but not the manner of her death.

The officer gave me a skeptical look but nodded for me to step into the van. I pulled the door closed behind me.

"Paxton," Malika was surprised but not entirely unhappy to see me. "What are you doing here? You're not working," she said as a statement, seeing I was not in uniform.

"No, I was just down the street at a Bats game. I knew you'd be here for this. Wow, you look great."

She ignored that last bit. "This? How did you know about this? The press just got the story," she said pointing to one of the TV monitors.

I looked right into those big, brown-green eyes and smiled. I said, "Hi, I'm Vulcan."

CHAPTER THIRTY-FOUR

Any question about whether Malika Kelly was in the loop about mysterious 911 calls from somebody calling himself Vulcan, were put to rest in an instant. When she tensed, her gown slipped, revealing, not just the sculpted calf and well-turned ankle I was expecting, but a small pistol in an ankle holster. Sgt. Kelly stared at me for a long time and then reached for a remote on the small table next to her. Then she discretely covered her leg explaining, "I'm required to carry a gun when I'm on duty."

She pushed a couple of buttons on the remote and I saw a red light come on an electronic device in the console next to her. She was recording us.

"So, let's hear your story. Start with your name."

I laid out the whole story, from my divorce, the depression and drinking, buying the boat, the suicide attempt, the ECT and the flashes. From one pocket, I pulled out the burner phone with vellum taped over the microphone and from another pocket, the battery. I told her about the police presence on cell phones at Slugger Field and asked, "Were they tracking my signal or was that paranoia on my part?" Sgt. Kelly was all business and ignored my question. She asked me to tell her about each and every flash I could remember.

But before I could do that, I got another flash. I held up an index finger, silently requesting time. I assembled the phone, folded back the vellum, and dialed the three digits. I leaned in toward Malika so she could hear both sides of the conversation. Yes, I could have put the phone on speaker, but that wouldn't have gotten me closer to her. Eyes closed, I inhaled her perfume until from the phone I heard, "Well, if it isn't the Vulcan man. What have you done now?"

I ignored the accusation. "There's been a break-in at Bob's House of

Crap. Baxter Avenue and Breckenridge. Bob has a guard dog that is part bullmastiff, part garbage disposal and the dog has taken out a hunk of ass that used to belong to a Stan Weintraub. Mr. Weintraub is bleeding and is trapped in a closet." I hung up and pulled the battery.

Bob's House of Crap is a flea market. Bob Marshall is a curmudgeon who doesn't like anybody or anything. He was known for scowling at customers and throwing out anyone who tried to dicker on the price. And you could torture him within an inch of his life, and he would still never admit that he got the name for his store from an episode of 'Friends'. In naming his store, Bob was just going for truth in advertising but ended up with a brilliant business strategy which drew customers by the dozen. Then a story written without Bob's co-operation appeared in Southern Living Magazine. The piece featured a photo of Bob snarling at a customer so now people flocked in from as far as Florida. Many just want a selfie beneath the store's sign and some want to talk to Bob about franchising opportunities.

Malika turned up her police radio and we both listened as dispatch sent a police car and EMS to Bob's, "Code 2," in other words, hurry, but not too much.

By the time I had related everything about every flash I could recall, it was after midnight. I was exhausted. "And you can tell by the way the 9-1-1 operator took my call, they think I'm somehow involved in all these things I'm reporting."

Malika clicked the stop button on her remote. "Well, that's understandable. It is a pretty bizarre story." Then she put up both hands to stop me before I got defensive. "I believe you. We've been tracking the Vulcan calls and my lieutenant has a map in her office with colored pins highlighting your flashes. But this information is only available to a few people."

"Let's do this," she said looking at the blank wall in the back of the van, "go home, get some sleep, I'll do the same. Come into HQ in the morning, say around eight. That will give me time to grease some wheels, show this interview. We'll figure it out from there."

"You're going to let me go home?"

"I believe you Paxton."

"You won't get in trouble for letting me go?"

"Only if you don't show up tomorrow."

I nodded and relaxed in my chair. After a few seconds, "So, your big date got busted up tonight."

She looked up to the ceiling and rolled her eyes. "Yeah, no loss there. The jerk's a detective in homicide and tried to tell me to let somebody else handle the run because that's what he was going to do. We're no more than five minutes from the scene of a high-profile death and he wouldn't leave a party." She heaved a sigh and said, "I did make one good decision. Last week he was so excited about all the free bourbon that was going to be flowing tonight, I told him I'd be driving."

"Give me a ride to my car?" I asked.

"Sure, just let me get out of this," she said removing the uniform blouse and sending my heart rate up about 20 ticks.

When we stepped from the van, only the crime scene technicians and a single squad car remained.

Malika dropped me at my car, and I made my way home to Bloomers. As my head hit the pillow, my phone chirped with a text message that read, "L8R G8R?"

Greatly relieved of the burden of my secret, I replied, "ZZZZZZ"

CHAPTER THIRTY-FIVE

Not wanting to violate Malika's trust, even accidentally, I arrived at the LMPD headquarters twenty minutes early. I checked in with the desk sergeant and had barely sat down to wait when Malika came through a door I hadn't noticed near a corner of the room. She was wearing her whole uniform this morning. She greeted me warmly, shook my hand and showed me into the maze that is the Louisville Police Department. Up a set of stairs and at room 212, before Malika opened the door, out the side of her mouth, she said, "Brace yourself."

Inside 212 were a man and a woman. The man was wearing these god-awful red, black and yellow plaid pants and a fluorescent green polo shirt. I recognized his face from the news. The woman wore her dress blue uniform. "Paxton, this is Chief Baker-Brown and Lieutenant Heath."

"Mr. Gahl call me Roland," he said shaking my hand.

"Natalie Heath," said the woman as we shook.

"Pardon my outfit, I'm working a charity golf tournament this morning," said the chief. "I don't play golf, so they made me an honorary rules official with the emphasis on honorary. This outfit should give them an idea of how serious they should take my officiating. Sgt. Kelly has been briefing us this morning. This thing that has happened to you is quite bizarre Mr. Gahl, have you talked to your psychiatrist about this, uuh… development?"

"Call me Pax, Chief. No, I thought she might lock me up and throw away the key," I said.

"Well, there's no fear of that now. My officers have documented everything you've reported. I called your boss, Brenda Trainor, we know each other, of course. I briefed her and she'll co-operate any way she can." Looking to Malika, he said, "Sgt. Kelly could speak to your doctor to confirm your legitimacy if need be. See if she can shed some light."

"Excellent," I said.

"I'd like you to stress doctor-patient confidentiality. Who else knows about these flashes?"

"Just my EMT partner, Angela Barton," I said.

"Good," he turned to Lt. Heath. "Call Director Trainor and ask her to talk to Barton. I think we should keep this on a need-to-know." Turning back to me, "Do you have a problem with that."

"No, I'd prefer that myself."

"Great." He paused as if looking at a mental checklist. "We've been following this Vulcan character with interest of course, and Sgt. Kelly's interview has brought clarity. Lt. Heath and Sgt. Kelly have come up with a plan of how we can exploit this gift of yours to the benefit of the city. I think you'll like it. I just slapped my rubber stamp on Project Vulcan. The police department can pay you $200 a week for your trouble. Best we can do. Budget's always tight. I'll let them explain it all, I've got to be at the course for the 9 o'clock tee time."

Shaking my hand again he said, "Pax, we're glad to have you on-board. If you figure out why this is happening to you, I suggest you apply for a patent. This city could use another dozen Vulcans."

"So. Project Vulcan," said Lt. Heath. She dropped hard into a chair as soon as the Chief left the room. "We don't know what's happening here, so we want to document everything. The hope is that if we accumulate enough information, we'll be able to make some sense out of all this. Because nobody knows where all these flashes are coming from, we decided to look for any correlation we could find between where you were when you had a flash and where the incident took place."

Malika turned one of the two lap-top computers in my direction. It was then that I noticed how tired she looked. I realized they were both exhausted.

"Hey, have you two been at this all night? Malika, I mean Sgt. Kelly, did you even go home after you dropped me last night," I said.

"Of course, I went home. If you remember, I was wearing a gown when you saw me last."

"I'm not likely to forget,.."

Malika interrupted, "I sent Lt. Heath your interview and we met up at six to hack out a plan to present to the Chief."

"Let's make this easier by using first names," said Heath.

"We plotted your location on this map," Malika said pointing to the wall map of the city behind her. "You're the purple pins."

"And the white pins are where the incidents took place."

I held up an index finger as I assembled my burner phone.

Malika stopped me, "No, use this," she said as she pressed a single button on a new iPhone.

"Vulcan, good morning, what's the emergency." This dispatcher's tone was deferential.

"Uh, good morning. A caddy at Willow Creek Country Club named Dwight Turner has been hit in the head with a golf club by a James Dorsey. They're on the second tee. Dorsey is drunk, but this was not an accident."

Before I had finished, Heath and Kelly were sticking pins in the map and entering data on the lap top.

"Aaah yes, drunk at 9:00 in the morning and all I want is breakfast. That's not where the Chief was going is it, "said Malika.

"No, his thing is at Valhalla Golf Club," said Heath.

"Well, la-de-da. I hope he checked to see if they'd let him through the gate in that get-up," laughed Malika. Valhalla is an exclusive PGA course deep into that part of town I call Waylo.

Having a recent history of being drunk at nine in the morning, I tried to blend into the woodwork during this exchange.

Malika said, "So Pax that phone is yours to use as you see fit. The city is picking up the tab. Use it for all your Vulcan calls. The GPS will tell us where you were when you got the flash; we'll record a time stamp and incident location at dispatch. And you'll get premium 9-1-1 service by pushing just one button," Malika said.

"Ah, it's an energy saving device then," I said.

Malika picked up purple and white pins and stuck them into the wall map. She stared for a few seconds, said, "Hey," and continued to stare.

Heath said, "What do you see?"

"Probably nothing, I guess. But that golf course assault just now? I don't think Pax has ever been that far away from an incident."

"Oh really," Heath said getting up from her chair. "We need to add a new column to the spreadsheet that shows the distance from Vulcan to incident," said Heath.

She seemed to blush with ecstasy as her fingertips hovered over the keyboard. I knew that a lot of people liked spreadsheets, but Heath couldn't take her eyes off her computer.

"Wait, before you do that, how about breakfast on me," I said, "I just got a raise."

Malika said, "yes please," at precisely the moment Lt. Heath said "no thanks." Heath added," I'm going to massage these numbers some more, then I'm going home for a while." It was probably my imagination that her voice caressed the word 'massage.'

Walking out of HQ, Malika nixed the idea of eating breakfast at the place across from the police department, saying it was too much of a "cop shop."

"I try to avoid rooms packed with a lot of macho guys with guns. Too much testosterone and I'd be shaving my legs twice a day."

Lowering my voice as much as I could and hiking up my pants, I said, "Well, you'll be safe with me ma'am. You will never have to fear too much macho testosterone when I'm around." Malika did a 'catch and release' move on my elbow when she laughed. And I slapped a mental high-five.

CHAPTER THIRTY-SIX

Text from Pax: "Shock Wave"
    Text from Malika: "Of All the Gahl"

Sunday was spent in boat maintenance. Crunchy, as I was still calling him despite my best efforts, came by to offer his advice on repairing a door hinge on the cabin door and firming up a built-in chest-of-drawers. I admit the whole idea of doing maintenance work was palatable because it envisaged a trip to one of my favorite places, the hardware store. For me the right ingredients for a hardware store are: local owner whose first name is above the door, i.e. Keith's or Oscar's; owner-operator is older than dirt; narrow aisles; a million items of merchandise floor to ceiling; staff in jeans and plaid shirts and able to put their hands on exactly what you need while blind-folded.

While Crunchy and I were in Keith's trying to find just the right stainless-steel screw to fix the door hinge, I got a flash. As I reached for my new phone, I said to Cliff, "I'll explain this later."

"Hi, yeah, we've got an overdose, 621 Hickory Street in Germantown. The second-floor apartment. John Lapfeld. Heroin."

Outside the store I explained to Cliff about the flashes and fessed up to having instant knowledge about the girl who crashed her BMW the day he and the boys took me out for a milkshake.

"In hindsight, I had my first flash when you were driving me home from the hospital. We went past that pool hall on Market where a guy was getting the shit beat out of him. I didn't get freaked out until I saw the story on the news that night. It was just as if I'd been there and seen it."

"Seen or foreseen," asked Cliff.

"Seen. In real time, as far as we can tell."

"We?"

"I'm working with LMPD. And Malika Kelly," I said as I did the Groucho Marx eyebrow wink.

I had flashes before and after Crunchy and I ate lunch at Check's in the Schnitzelburg neighborhood. One was a domestic violence call and the other was another OD. It had been a chilly, rainy day and I wondered if there had been a survey done to find if chilly and rainy were ingredients that produced more domestic violence and drug overdoses.

Cliff, a man of science, used to dealing in absolutes, left me with, "This is some crazy shit Pax. I want to say, 'be careful,' but I don't know of what."

"Don't have to tell me it's crazy. Chief Baker-Brown said to keep this on the Q.T. Information about the flashes is on a need-to-know basis." Telling Cliff didn't count, the man was a vault. "He thinks we may find a way to better exploit this thing. But my girlfriend, that would be Malika Kelly, the Police Public Information Officer…"

I paused here for a moment to give Cliff time to roll his eyes and shout," You haven't even had a date, for Christ's sake."

"We're going out Friday night," I said trying again at the Groucho eyebrow thing.

"Malika reminded me that the Chief is a political appointee. He loves the quick arrests and response times but he's also gonna' want to cover his ass."

It was time for Cliff to raise his eyebrows. "Did she tell you that?" asked Cliff.

I just smiled and nodded.

"Maybe you're not delusional, maybe she really does like you," he said opening his eyes wide in mock wonder.

CHAPTER THIRTY-SEVEN

Text from Malika: "The 2B Announced"
Text from Pax: "H2O House"

Monday morning found me in the basement of Brown Cancer Center getting fitted for a mask and a lead shield. Radiation treatments would start the next day. The mask was for targeting purposes. X-ray radiation kills cancer cells and by having a precise target for the x-ray machine, there is less collateral damage to normal cells. A fluorescent-green thermo-plastic mesh was taken from a vat of warm water and was then stretched over my face and fastened down to the table I was lying on. I was ordered by the technician to lie still for 20 minutes while the mesh hardened. I was awakened by the radiologist when she was marking a spot on the mask and my cheek with a black Sharpie. It would be locked in place to the table to immobilize my head during treatments. Any movement could throw the radiation off target.

The techs would touch-up their artwork on my face every day to make sure it stayed on if I happened to bathe in the next 24 hours. On Fridays, they would double-up the marks to make sure the target lasted through the weekend. So many people have tattoos, I didn't feel too conspicuous. The tech told me one of her co-workers was taking an art class to get better at her Sharpie work. She thought the patients would feel more comfortable with something that looked like a tattoo rather than a radiation target.

A dentist made a wax mold of my teeth and cast a model in hard acrylic that contained a small lead shield that was to protect my teeth and gums from the radiation that was aimed at a small area on my cheek.

Radiation would take a few minutes each day with Saturdays and Sundays off. Chemotherapy would be every Friday and take half the morning. After five weeks of radiation, I would not have to shave my right cheek ever again and the skin would remain as soft and smooth as a woman's breast.

I wasn't surprised, that morning, to get a text message from psychiatrist Dr. Karen Newman, informing me that I was expected in her office at 9AM. Once again, the message didn't offer a way to reject the invitation, but I was anxious to make this particular appointment because I planned to be asking more questions than I answered. The evening before, I had declined Malika's offer to accompany me in full police regalia to vouch for my sanity. I traded a date to the doctor's office for a real date to dinner. I was so smooth.

After the preliminaries were finished and I established an absence of depression (Did I mention I'd just made a date with a beautiful woman?), I began.

"Have you ever encountered, in the literature or in practice, any unusual side-effects as a result of shock treatments?"

"What kind of side-effects," she said.

"I'm asking the questions here sister!" Ok, I didn't say that out loud.

"Let's try this, tell me how these ECTs normally go," I said.

"The average number of ECTs is between six and twelve and 70% of the time a person in a severe state of depression will be relieved. It is very unusual that a patient gets only one treatment like you did, but it's not unheard of. Last week, I had a patient who was catatonic. Do you know what that is?"

"Yeah, they're rigid, staring off into space," I ventured.

"Yes, muscular rigidity, awake, unresponsive and in a stupor. When he woke up from an ECT, he looked at me, smiled and said, 'Hey, Dr. Newman, how are you.' Now that is unusual."

With knitted brows, she said, "Paxton, what's this about?"

So, I was about half-way through my story about the flashes when I said, "Ah, a concrete illustration." This was, in fact, the second flash of the day. The first one had woken me at two in the morning. Douglas Bligh had his third and last DUI when he crashed thru a guardrail on River Road and ended upside down in the Ohio River.

I pulled my new cell phone from my pocket, held it so Newman could see the LMPD logo on the back of the case and hear the conversation. I pushed that single button.

"9-1-1, what's your....oh, Vulcan, what's up?"

"Yeah, hi, a psych patient at University Hospital just injured a nurse in the ER. No need to send anyone, hospital security is on it and the nurse is being looked at. Chief Baker-Brown wants everything documented, so I thought it best to call anyway." This last part was for the benefit of Dr. Newman.

"Roger that. Vulcan, what are the names and what was the injury?"

"The nurse is Bill James. He has a broken right rib. The patient is a frequent flier to the psych unit. They have him listed as John Doe 47, but his first name is Evan."

Newman looked a little dumb-founded and I gave her a minute to absorb what she'd just heard. "So, these flashes are always the same kind of things I encounter as an EMT, except I know about them as soon as they happen. So, why is this happening?"

She said, "I don't know," but she had a look on her face that I couldn't identify.

I thought to myself, "But you do know something."

"Let's try this," I said. "Give me the whole blow by blow account of my ECT, I was really out of it and remember nothing."

Now I could see she was nervous, she looked at the floor and ran her fingers through her hair before she said, "Ok, well, when we got the green light to go ahead with the ECT, I asked you to lie down on the gurney. You sat staring at a blank wall for a while and the third time I asked you, you complied. I gave you a shot of succinylcholine," she said.

"Succinylcholine is a general anesthetic and muscle relaxant. Once you were asleep, we put light restraints on your legs and a padded tongue depressor in your mouth. My assistant attached an EKG to your chest and some conductive paste on each side of your forehead. I picked up the two wands of the ECT machine...." Here I stopped her.

"What's that like?"

Newman hesitated while she tried to decide whether she should tell me. "Well one of the nurses calls it the toaster but we're trying to break him of that."

"Perfect," I laughed.

Newman added, "It's about the size of a four-slice toaster with a few dials and switches on the side."

"Anyway, wands against your forehead I trigger a pulse. Your feet jiggled a little, your EKG did a little dance. All perfectly normal," she added quickly. "You blushed a bright red and then you slept. For the next ten hours. That part is a bit unusual, but you were exhausted."

I was convinced by now that something about this had been different. I said, "Is there anything that wasn't normal or routine?"

Dr. Newman shifted uncomfortably in her chair. She looked down at her feet like she was thinking. I knew she'd made a decision when she looked out the window. She turned and looked me in the eye. "You may have had a concussion from your suicide attempt. If you did then it would have been advisable to wait on the ECT." She breathed a sigh of relief.

I waited.

"A concussion can be hard to diagnose if a patient is unconscious or uncooperative. You fell into the second category. I interviewed you looking for any retrograde amnesia. Post-traumatic amnesia is the primary indicator for the prognosis of a concussion, but it is dependent on the patient answering questions. Like what's the last play you remember before you were tackled. All your answers were, 'I don't care.'"

Newman picked up her computer tablet and scrolled through it. "When you were brought in, you had many symptoms of a concussion: grogginess, confusion, sensitivity to light and noise, problems with balance, headache, nausea, but these are also symptoms of someone who's drunk. And there is no question that you were drunk."

"No, there was no question about that," I agreed.

"You were stone cold sober when we gave you the ECT a couple of days later, but you continued to say you didn't care about anything."

"Look, I'm not blaming you, I'm just trying to understand what's going on."

"I'll do some research," Newman said, "and in the meantime, I'd like to see you more often." Punching at her tablet, she brightened. "Friday mornings, you're in chemotherapy. You'll be a captive audience for five weeks. That's perfect; I'll drop by."

"During my chemo? Won't I be asleep?"

Dr. Newman looked down at her tablet again. "No, you're getting a low dose of chemo, you'll have a sedative, but I'll keep you awake long enough to check-in with you, see how you're doing."

A thought crossed my mind. I stared her down and she looked away.

"You're thinking of making a case study of me, aren't you," I asked.

Newman blanched and then brightened. "How,.... Did you know what I was thinking, did you get a flash?"

"No, no, just my normal brilliance. You want to get a research paper out of this, don't you?"

Newman didn't look away this time. "Would that be a problem?"

"If you write this up, I have some conditions."

Cautious now, Newman asked, "What conditions?"

"You don't use real names on these medical studies, right?"

"Correct."

"Here's a couple of other items that might not be real. Subject was male, 6-foot 3 inches tall, 190 pounds and in robust physical condition."

She looked me up and down, frowned and said, "Ok, I don't see the harm there."

Now feeling my oats. I gave her a steely look, "And you have to use this exact phrase, "He is hung like a race-horse.""

CHAPTER THIRTY-EIGHT

Text from Pax: "Secretariat"
Text from Malika: "????"

The only thing difficult about my radiation treatment was the waiting room. It took longer to don the mouth guard and mask and then remove said equipment than the treatment took. There was no pain. My time in the waiting room was never long, and sometimes I didn't even sit down. In that waiting room were women and men whose cancer wasn't obvious, but some had been horribly disfigured by the cancer or subsequent surgery to remove it.

There are a lot of cancer patients out there in the world, and by necessity, the radiation therapy department is run like a well-oiled machine. We were all on a rigid schedule of appointments and we would see each other every day at the same time. After a few days, I made it a point to say "Good Morning" to the room of five or six people. And every day, I wished there'd been a separate exit door so I could by-pass that waiting room on my way out.

And, of course, I thought there but for the grace of dog...Yes, dog, not god. I'm not religious and every time I think of that 'there but for the grace' cliché, the next thought is of that old joke about what happens if you're a dyslexic, agnostic, insomniac. Answer: You stay awake at night wondering if there really is a dog. For me, it's like a song that I hear and then can't get it out of my head. An earworm.

The joke has caused me plenty of embarrassment because I think of the punchline and I will smile inappropriately. Like at the homeless guy with his hand out on the sidewalk. Or at the drunk, on crutches trying to get through a revolving door. I'm ashamed. Fortunately, this hasn't been a problem at work. At work, in an emergency situation, I manage to stay focused on the job.

In the effort to keep knowledge of the flashes in a closed loop, Director Trainor saw to it that Angela and I were partnered together on a permanent basis. We started our regular shift at 6AM and at 8, Angela would park the 'bone box' outside the Jackson Street entrance to the Brown Cancer Center while I went inside for my 15-minute radiation treatment.

Every Monday, either Sgt. Kelly or Lt. Heath would call and arrange to rendezvous with Angela and me for lunch. It was at that first lunch at a restaurant called Ditto's in the Highlands that Heath, her laptop open on the table, showed us what she'd found.

"There is a clear trend," she said. "Two things are happening. You are having more flashes and the radius, with you in the center, is expanding."

My first thought was surprise, but then there was the second thought.

"I'm not having to sneak around anymore. There is a lot less effort involved in calling these in now, so I guess I didn't notice making more calls. How many more?"

"Four more calls last week than the week before." And anticipating my next question Heath added, "A quarter mile larger radius."

"Ah, well, that's not much," said Angela.

"But it is," said Malika sitting up straight next to me in the booth. "That means a half mile diameter increase in a week."

My first date with Malika a few days before had gone very well. We'd gone to dinner at a sushi place and talked so much we found we didn't have time to take in the movie we planned on. At dinner, I fell in love with her laugh.

In her persona as police information officer, the public never saw a smile let alone heard a laugh. Her time spent in front of the TV cameras was to deliver news of death, injury or malfeasance. Arrest announcements too were somber events because they carried with them tragedies that brought us there. Off the clock, Malika loved to laugh, and that laugh became my favorite sound.

After dinner we went back to Bloomers and soaked in the cool clear evening on the top deck with coffee and a Japanese dessert of mochi we'd brought from the restaurant. The evening was broken up by the second flash of the night, a welder burned by hot slag while working the night shift at the barge building company directly across the river from where we sat. We turned in our seats and waited until the red flashing lights from an ambulance ricocheted across the waves toward us. The sirens didn't reach us.

After walking Malika from the docks to her van we dug in for some passionate kissing when she suddenly broke it off and asked, "What's with the name Secretariat for the boat?"

I was grateful for the darkness as I felt myself blush. I stammered, "aaa, I was reaching a bit on that one, it has to do with going the distance, giving it all I've got. It's a bit of a stretch."

I could not so much see as feel the skepticism on her face, but she let it pass. After another long kiss, she said, "Speaking of horses, are you busy around 6AM Sunday morning?"

"Never," I protested.

"The ponies are running at Churchill Downs; they're hosting the Breeders' Cup and I can get us into the backside. They do early morning workouts and it's fun to be up close enough to touch these incredible thoroughbreds." Then, as if she didn't know I was thrilled to be going out with her for a second time, she added, "There will be breakfast."

"Ahh, there it is, you buried the lead, officer," I said as I wrapped my arms around her.

We kissed again, and when my hands went looking for redemption, Malika pushed me away with a laugh and said, "I'll pick you up right here at 5:40, we'll need the police van to get through the gate."

As she got behind the wheel, I said, "You know, you could just stay on the boat tonight, there's plenty of room."

"Where would you sleep," she asked with a mischievous smile.

"Well, I..."

"Good night, Paxton. I had a great time," she said as she started her van.

CHAPTER THIRTY-NINE

I was never so happy to wake up at 5 on a Sunday morning. By 5:40 I was showered, shaved and had downed a cup of black coffee. Not wanting to disturb the total quiet, I stepped softly across the wooden docks and up the metal stairs to the Knights of Columbus parking lot where I waited for Malika. Walking across the two lanes of River Road is commonly a death-defying act, but not early on a Sunday morning. A gray mist blanketed the river. Silently emerging from that shroud was a long barge pushing upriver against the current. As I watched, sunrise struck the top of our tallest skyscraper downtown, five miles west. Once again, the building's penthouse residents would get more of the day as they were the first to greet the sun and the last to see it go. The scene was tranquility itself.

Before I saw it, I heard Malika's unmarked police van from a half mile off. I climbed into the passenger seat and she leaned over to meet me halfway for a morning kiss.

"Hey," I said, "you look even more fabulous than usual. Do I need to go back and put on some slacks or something?" I was in black jeans and running shoes, she was in dress slacks, a navy polo shirt with the LMPD logo and fancy boots.

"No, you're fine, I may have some work to do. Local networks and some radio stations are set up along the back stretch and I could get pulled in to say hello. Security is always an issue when there are big crowds and valuable thoroughbreds at Churchill, so if I get a chance, I'd like to remind the public that the LMPD is on the job."

An LMPD officer was on duty at the gate, so Malika didn't need to flash her badge, only her smile. The backside of Churchill Downs is a busy place. There are dozens of barns and perhaps a thousand horses. More than 600 people, from ten or twelve countries, care for the horses and live above the stables.

Into my phone, I said, "Churchill Downs," my 911 calls were evolving into shorthand. "Backside, barn 12, stable-hand, Arlin Perez, broken ribs, unconscious, knocked into a wall by the horse he was grooming, on my way there myself."

Malika listened to my call without comment and then jogged along beside me until she spotted a uniformed LMPD officer. Malika issued instructions for him to direct EMS to barn 12.

The jog through the people, horses and buildings of the backside reminded me that I needed to start running again. It was at least a quarter mile jog to barn 12. When I got there, I was out of breath and had trouble asking the first person I saw, "Where's Arlin?"

"Eh," said the very short, brown skinned woman.

"Arlin, Arlin Perez? Aqui?" I said, pointing to the barn and using up all of my Spanish in one word.

"Ah, si," she said as she led me into the barn.

Mr. Perez, who was beginning to wake up when we arrived, lay crumpled in the straw at the feet, or rather hoofs, of a beautiful bay horse named War Monger. Maybe the name was meant as a warning shot to anyone in the vicinity, but the stable hand with us was not deterred. She roughly pushed on the hind quarters of the horse to get him away from Perez all the while firing off a verbal fusillade that made War Monger give her a blank look that said, 'what is your problem.'

Perez had one hand on his chest, the other on his head as he started to get up.

"Wait, Mr. Perez," I said.

Turning to the woman I said, with words and sign language, "Can we get this horse out of here?"

She understood instantly and led the horse out of the stall.

I told Arlin Perez, "I'm with EMS, can I examine you?"

He started to nod but winced at the movement he made.

Feeling the knot at the back of his head, but not finding blood, I unsnapped his western style plaid shirt to look at his chest for bruising. Without a stethoscope to determine if a broken rib had punctured a lung, I watched his chest rise and fall as he breathed. Seeing nothing amiss there, I started to prod the area Perez had been protecting. But then reminded myself that I already knew Perez had a broken rib and there was no need to inflect more pain. About then, the cavalry arrived in the form of John Cobbs and Gary Findling.

"I must be seeing double," I said, "two paramedics riding together?"

"When the horses are running, we volunteer for this post. What have we got?" Gary said, getting to business.

"Arlin Perez," I started.

"How you know my name is Arlin? Everybody calls me 'A', I don't like 'Arlin,'" he said.

I looked around the barn mystified. "I must have seen your name somewhere. Anyway, 'A' Perez here was unconscious when we arrived, knot on the back of the head, and broken rib." As soon as I said this, I realized my mistake. "I'm just guessing on the rib." Turning back to Perez, "you'll need an X-ray before we know for sure."

Resuming our walk to the media tents, Malika said, "Well, with a broken rib, he won't be grooming horses for a while."

"No." Then I decided to show off a little, "But maybe he could be a hot-walker."

She turned to me and smiled, "Ok, I'll bite, what's a hot-walker."

"These big machines," I said pointing to a gray horse being led past us to the track, "need to be walked for 30 minutes after a training run to cool them down. That will probably be good for Mr. Perez's ribs too since there's not much else to do for broken ribs."

The media tents were set up cheek to jowl along the back stretch, just like vendors set up their tents at craft fairs. The difference was that the TV personalities had their backs to all the folks wandering past them or leaning against the rail to get a better look at thoroughbred workouts. The cameras were trained toward the "on air" talent and over their shoulders in the frame were the twin spires of Churchill Downs. As TV and radio people did their shows, horses galloped by in the background and "owners" milled about.

The owners of racehorses can encompass several economic tiers. You can own the whole horse outright; you can share ownership with several others or there is the way Cliff did it. The only economical way for the average joe to own a racehorse is to buy a small share with lots of other people. If you are very lucky, your horse will finish in the money sometimes, thereby offsetting some of the expenses of paying people like 'A' Perez to house, feed, train and doctor your horse. And let's not forget transportation cost from one racetrack to another. A charter flight for a horse can be $5,000.

Cliff was one of 200 who put down $500 for a share in a syndicate. If you're a fan of horseracing, this is like having front row season tickets to a Big Ten university basketball program. The legendary trainer, D. Wayne Lucas, chose the thoroughbred to purchase, train and race. For their investment, the 200 get access to horse and trainer, free admission and parking to Churchill and a D. Wayne Lukas bobblehead. Usually, racehorses win little or nothing and the owners are on the hook for all the bills. For years.

Remembering this, I told Malika, walking beside me, "My friend Cliff had part ownership in a horse once. He felt really bad the day the horse broke his leg and had to be put down. He felt bad that the animal must have been in pain. He didn't feel bad about not having to write that check every month."

During commercial breaks, Malika made her presence known to the media and several asked her to sit in for short interviews. I watched from the sidelines in awe at how comfortable she was in front of the cameras. I called in a double overdose of two friends who needed to start off their morning with a shot of heroin. And I called in a domestic in which the husband, Joshua Hughes, thought he'd begin this fine day by beating the shit out of his common-law wife Sigrid Johnson. Did he wonder at finding the police and EMS pounding at his door, demanding to be let in when Sigrid hadn't made so much as a sound when he cold-cocked her, sending her, not for the first time, to never-never land? I began to wonder how many of the 911 calls I was making, would never have been made at all.

After the interviews, Malika and I rested our arms atop the backstretch rail. In companionable silence, we watched as the scattered clouds parted and the sun illuminated the carefully groomed dirt and turf tracks of the Downs.

After a while, Malika said, "Alright, how about some breakfast?"

"Let's eat," I said.

I started in the direction of a sign I'd seen for "Track Kitchen," but Malika took my arm and held on as she steered me toward the van.

"The food isn't anything special there, let's go to Wagner's Pharmacy, better food, china plates and cups." Her arm in mine was a good feeling.

"My treat," she said.

CHAPTER FORTY

Breakfast was interrupted twice with flashes. Big events at Churchill like the Derby and the Breeders' Cup can draw over 150,000 race fans and the locals would prefer to drive their own cars. Homeowners around the Downs turn their yards into parking lots and rent out parking spaces. The first breakfast flash came about when two visitors vying for the last spot in a prime front yard lot came to blows. The second call was an injury accident. With both calls, I had to excuse myself from the table in order to make the calls in privacy. Most of my flashes on this morning were to streets I wasn't familiar with. I didn't know how far away they were.

When I returned from the second call, Malika said, "Next time we'll need to pick a restaurant where the tables are farther apart so you can have some privacy. But you're busier than usual, aren't you?"

"Yeah, you're right. And I was just thinking that I could skip the injury accident calls because there's almost always a cell phone hero to call it in. But the truth is, timing is crucial. An injury accident can become a fatal one in seconds. Sorry, I'm preaching to the choir."

In general, people want to help their fellows but are often conflicted about getting involved. It works something like this: "9-1-1, what's your emergency?"

Cellphone hero: "Yeah, there's this guy laying on the sidewalk and there's a lot of blood."

911: "What's the location?"

Cellphone hero: "141 Chenoweth Lane." Then click and they hang up.

After breakfast, as Malika was stowing her credit card, she said, "Hey, how about taking me for a boat ride."

"On my boat,....War Monger?" I said.

"On your boat,....Gahl's Gondola," she said.

I waited until we were standing on the dock in front of Bloomers to confess to Malika that I'd driven my own boat only once. I enjoyed her laugh even if it was at my expense.

"Hello neighbor," came from Celia Shepard as she and Bob came down the steps to the dock on their return from church.

I introduced Malika and asked the Shepards if I could get a lesson on the operation of my Kingscraft 34 Coastal Cruiser. I fought the chauvinistic impulse to look at Bob when I asked the question.

"You haven't had her out in a while have you," said Bob.

"No sir, not since I took ownership," I said. "I could use a refresher."

"Won't be a minute, I need to change clothes because we have to go down in your engine compartment to check a few things before we fire her up."

Bob Shepard was like a kid in a candy store or me in a hardware store, as he showed me how to check fluids, do a visual inspection of hoses and look for water leaks. I heard Malika and Celia Shepard talking and laughing above, caught the word, "postcard" and knew they were discussing the inscription in French on the back of the framed card on the wall that I still hadn't bothered to translate.

After Malika's first visit to Bloomers, I'd been embarrassed enough about displaying photos of half-naked women to flip the frames over. I'd bought reversible frames with glass on both sides and now the exposed side showed the addressee, the message and stamp. All in French.

After the engine compartment passed visual inspection, Bob directed me to the helm. He had me flip on the toggle that ran a blower that sucks any gas fumes out of the engine compartment. Trial and error have shown that removing the gas fumes is an excellent way to keep the boat from exploding when the engine ignition switch is turned. After letting the blower run for a couple of minutes, Bob said, "Ok, fire it up."

Bloomers did not disappoint. After a brief crank of the key, the engine came to life and idled smoothly. While we let the motor warm up, Bob explained the various gauges and levers and recommended we start out down river toward downtown Louisville so that on our return, I would have plenty of time to get used to steering against the current by the time I needed to dock back at K of C. Before he left, and without a word, Bob wrote his cell number and handed it to me.

After I disconnected the K of C power and water lines, Bob and Celia took up positions at the bow lines while Malika released both stern lines. At my thumbs up to the Shepards, they released the ropes from their cleats and shoved Bloomers away from the dock. I shifted into reverse and backed out smoothly like I knew what I was doing. Malika came to stand beside me. "Hey, this is sorta fun."

"You might want to hold off on that kind of talk until we get back in one piece," I said.

But it was a great training run for a newbie. There were no barges or giant steamboats to dodge, it was still before noon on a Sunday morning and the river-rats were sleeping it off and hadn't yet taken to their speedboats and jet-skis. Our turn-around point was the 2nd Street bridge, known to Google map users everywhere as the George Rogers Clark Memorial Bridge. Clark was given credit for founding Louisville but was eclipsed by his little brother Bill who got his name on a famous trek called the Lewis and Clark Expedition.

Malika's confidence in my seamanship was growing along with mine. And when we again crossed under the Big Four Bridge, she went up to the top deck and exchanged waves with the walkers 50 feet above us. The Big Four was an abandoned railroad bridge that was recently put to great use as a walking bridge. Day and night, winter and summer, someone is always walking the Big Four.

When she came back inside, Malika said, "How about a picnic lunch on Six Mile Island?"

"Ok, let's do it. See what you can find to eat."

Six Mile Island, so named because it's that far from downtown Louisville, is a nature preserve of about 80 acres. Accessible only by boat, it is not someplace you would want to be when the Ohio is at flood stage. Even though it's much closer to the Indiana shore, Kentucky's boundary-line is at that shore, so Six Mile is Kentucky property.

I saw no other boats as we approached the island and didn't take my eyes off the water as I looked for rocks, stickups and floating debris. I could hear Malika moving about in the kitchen behind me and I shouted over my shoulder, "Land Ho."

Malika joined me at the wheel. She was barefoot, her pants legs were rolled up to her knees and she had changed into one of my extra-large, white T-shirts. She had gathered the shirt at the bottom and tied in a knot at her waist. She said, "I hope you don't mind."

"No," I said quickly. And after further consideration, I elaborated, "Uh, no."

Malika said, "I'll look for a place to land," kissed me on the cheek, and walked out on the bow deck.

I couldn't take my eyes off her as walked to the point of the bow and looked for a place for me to shove the keel into the soft mud. As we touched ground and I throttled forward another foot and then cut the engine. Malika was leaning over to tie the boat to a tree branch when I came out on deck. I stood back to enjoy the view. She took my hand and led me back inside the cabin. Two hours later, we got around to lunch.

CHAPTER FORTY-ONE

Text from Malika: "Ms. Bliss"
 Text from Pax: "Simply Irresistible"

The part that I left out from the boat ride, the part that I'm willing to share that is, was that the closer we got to the area of greater population density, with downtown Louisville to the south and Jeffersonville, Indiana to the north, the more flashes I had. There were six flashes in the short time we were in the area. Two of those were injuries suffered by wrestlers on the WWE Smackdown circuit. These were real injuries! They had arrived at the KFC YUM! Center where they would be performing that afternoon, to look over the venue.

The KFC YUM! Center is the home of the University of Louisville Cardinals basketball team. The building looks vaguely familiar to everyone who sees it for the first time, though they may not figure out why. The local folk lore on how the design came about has it that an intern for an architectural firm sat at his drafting table hunched over his sketch pad. He tapped his mechanical pencil, trying to focus on the job at hand. Everyone in the office had been asked to spitball ideas for this new arena. Skimming his eyes around the office, his glance landed on the new copier that was just delivered that morning. The copier was a 'state of the art', Consumer Reports 'Best Buy.' He sees his boss prowling the hallway and, in an effort to look busy, he begins to sketch the copier on his pad. In ten minutes, he is pleased with his rough sketch. As he is nodding his satisfaction, his eyes meet those of his boss across the room. The boss begins to walk in his direction. Quickly, this intern drew in roads on three sides of the copier and a river on the fourth side. He is erasing the word "Canon" and printing, KFC YUM! Center, as the boss reaches his desk.

The wrestlers' injuries came about over a disagreement about whose turn it was to win the afternoon match. Contracts were pulled from briefcases and thrust into faces. Fists into faces came next and then they both went for a head-butt at the same time. Two knockouts, two concussions.

A fourth flash was a guy who had overdosed on heroin. Rather than call 911, his girlfriend and her sister had managed to get his pants off him and set his butt in their kids wading pool. They had then emptied their icemaker and that of the neighbors across the hall, pouring ice on his nether regions. This is a recipe only for blue balls but there is a persistent myth in the drug world that this will cure an overdose. Another myth is that if the person is snoring, they're OK. This is not only wrong; it might be dead wrong.

So, I was happy to turn the boat around and head back east and our rendezvous with Six Mile. That afternoon, Six Mile Island became a special place for Malika and me.

CHAPTER FORTY-TWO

Monday morning, I was into the new routine. Angela and I started our shift at 6, radiation at 8 and at noon we met Lt. Natalie Heath and Sgt. Malika Kelly at Ditto's Grill for lunch for the weekly Project Vulcan check-in. After we'd ordered, Heath showed us her digital version of the map back at headquarters, lots of dots instead of pins. I immediately thought of Geocaching.

Geocaching.com bills itself as the world's largest treasure hunt. With an app on your smart phone, you can download caches, places where others playing the game have hidden trinkets and logbooks in caches. The GPS in your phone will direct you to the cache, often a small Tupperware container or ammo can, hidden in parks, in bushes or under park benches. Caches are found all over the world. There are over 3800 in the Louisville area alone. Cliff and I had been caching a few times and I found the ingenuity in hiding caches was remarkable. The Project Vulcan map wasn't a Geocache map yet, but the dots on my map were increasing every day.

The week went smoothly. On a day when Angela and I were posted downtown and had a break, we stopped by the communication office where the 911 dispatchers do their heroic work. We put faces to voices. EMTs and dispatchers have a lot in common, but I think dispatchers sometimes have the tougher job. For instance, by the time we get to a home where there's been a shooting or a drug overdose, the police have arrived and secured the scene. The dispatcher may have been on the phone with the victim's child trying to reassure them as they scream over the body of their parent.

Most dispatchers have had to try to talk down people calling to say 'goodbye' to someone before they take their life. Some have had to listen as people burn to death when trapped in a burning house or car. Compassion fatigue is very real among dispatchers. Vulcan was making their jobs just a little easier.

As we were taking our leave, I got a flash on an injury accident. Standing in that room, I had the sudden realization that the fastest response time would come if this is where I was when I got a flash. With the range of the flashes growing, I knew the number of incidents would be growing at an alarming rate. As we left, I made the prediction to Angela that this is where I would be working in a few weeks.

The hardest part of every day was getting my mouth open wide enough to get my acrylic covered lead guard in and out before and after radiation treatments. The easiest part of every day was crawling into bed with Malika every night.

Sunday evening after our day at the Downs and the boat ride to Six Mile Island, Malika had gone home exhausted. As I kissed her goodnight at her van, I suggested she should bring a change of clothes or two and stay awhile. She vowed to do just that. And she did.

The following week was a bit different. Once again, the range of the flashes had increased by a quarter mile. That was no longer a surprise. But what came next was a surprise.

"We want you to move," said Heath.

"Move? Move what," I said. I looked at Malika. The placid look on her face told me she wasn't hearing anything new.

"Move from where you live to someplace more central to the population density of the city. It's like you're the center of a radar screen. As the radar sweeps around there is a green blip every time you get a flash."

"So, if I lived in a more central location, I could report more flashes." I said.

Natalie Heath and Malika nodded.

"24/7," I said.

They nodded again.

"There is a city owned marina right downtown," I said thinking out loud.

"No, then you'd be getting flashes from southern Indiana cities," said Heath.

"And that would be wrong because…"

"Because you don't work for them," said Heath. And, realizing how that sounded, she added, "and the river is a mile wide and represents a big blank place for flashes."

"Chief Baker-Brown really likes all the great response times," said Malika. "Over-dose deaths are down, and arrest numbers are up because of you. My office has a history of publishing those numbers every month and the press has noticed. We told them we had been focusing attention on shaving off every second possible from our response time. And that's true, by the way."

"So, tell me, where would a more central, population density location be," I said. "And is there a boat dock?"

"The more central location would be near the University of Louisville, main campus," said Heath.

"No boat dock," said Malika, "but you could live with me."

CHAPTER FORTY-THREE

Text from Malika: "Home Sweet Home?"
Text from Pax: "Two Cozy"

The caller I.D. read, "Dorothy Koenig." The name rang a distant bell, so I answered.

"Paxton Gahl," I said.

"Mr. Gahl, this is Sarah Koenig, I'm the bank attorney that represented Althea Threadgill on the sale of her husband's boat, Bloomers." Her tone had more of a flavor of pleading than demanding, so I relaxed a bit.

"I remember Ms. Koenig; how can I help you?"

"May I come to see you? It is a matter of some delicacy and I'd rather see you in person, if I may."

"Can you give me an idea of what this is about," I said.

"Well, it's….," and then realizing what might be going through my head at the moment, she said, "Oh, it's nothing to do with the sale of the boat, there are no problems with any of that. This is all about Mr. Threadgill."

"Ok then, when and where would you like to meet?"

"Tonight, on Bloomers?"

"I'm at the Knights of Columbus dock. I'll be home by 5:30," I said

I gave Malika a heads-up about Sarah Koenig and she agreed to join the party.

When Koenig arrived, she was surprised, and not in a good way, to see Malika. But she rallied and as soon as she sat down, she opened her briefcase and laid out two sheets of paper on the coffee table between us.

"What's this," I said.

"It's a non-disclosure agreement." Koenig was well trained in the art of engaging a person in conversation. She looked you in the eye when she spoke. With the two of us sitting across from her on the couch, her gaze swung back and forth between us with a cadence that matched the pace of her speech. "Like I told Paxton on the phone," she said addressing Malika, "this has nothing to do with him, it's about Mr. Threadgill and the bank." Bouncing back and forth between us, she continued, "but what I must tell you is very sensitive and could be damaging to Mrs. Threadgill and the bank if this information gets out."

"Curiouser, and curiouser," I said. Malika and I picked up the sheets of paper like fish nibbling at a juicy nightcrawler. I did better at feigning disinterest. Malika signed first.

With paperwork filed away, Koenig sat back and told the unfinished tale of Norman Threadgill. He married money but the new wife came with a catch. He had to go into the family business. He was expected to work at the bank. William J. Powell II was Althea Threadgill's grandfather, and the bank's founder. And one day when his father-in-law was ready to step down, Norman would run the bank. Althea's father had but two expectations of his only child. She would marry a man who could run the bank when the time came, and she would propagate a son who could be made ready for his turn.

Norman started at the bottom of the banking ladder and worked his way up through every job in the bank, getting a boost by his father-in-law at every rung. The plot began to thicken early on when Norman was put in charge of the safe deposit boxes.

Mr. Threadgill was in that position during the momentous month of October 1987. In the first two weeks of that month, the stock market fell by 15%. On October 19, also known as Black Monday, the market fell another 22.6%. It was the second largest one-day stock market drop in U.S history.

In times of financial distress, people don't want a stock certificate that is suddenly worth half of what it had been the month before. They want something tangible they can hold in their hand. A safety net investment that is easily bought and sold. They buy gold. Gold ingots and gold coins. And whether the coins carry the profile of Lady Liberty, a soaring American Eagle or a South African Springbok they are beautiful to behold. Then there is a scramble for some place safe to put the gold. They go to their bank and rent a safe deposit box. October of 1987 was no exception. For weeks after Black Monday, Norman would carry the long, slim, empty boxes to the private cubicles where his customer waited and, in a few minutes, he would be summoned to return the now heavier boxes. No one told Norman what they'd put in their boxes, but Norman knew they were bringing him their gold. In 1987 the price of gold went up 25% over the year before and it would be 18 years before the price of an ounce of gold was ever that high again.

A week before Black Monday, Isadore Kosta had seen the writing on the country's financial wall and had taken action. On Tuesday, October 13, 1987, Kosta walked into Origins Bank and Trust carrying a briefcase. Mr. Kosta was listing to port as he walked in the double doors and the fingers of his left hand were white with the strain of the heavy case. Norman Threadgill's father-in-law, William Powell III, sitting in his glass walled office, sprang to attention as Kosta entered the building. Mr. Kosta, a hydraulic engineer with dozens of patents, was a valued customer.

After a brief introduction to Norman, Kosta abruptly handed him the briefcase. The shock of the sudden weight brought Norman to one knee, causing Kosta to double over with laughter. That was Kosta's first good laugh of the day, the second would come when Norman showed Isadore Kosta his box number. It was 1929.

Ms. Koenig's story had held me in rapt silence until now. I leapt to a theory. My voice hit some notes I hadn't heard since puberty. "The gold disappeared! You think it's on this boat?"

"I must be clear that Kosta heirs claim there was gold in the box. No one at the bank, of course, has ever seen the inside of the box," she said.

"No one still alive you mean." I was enjoying this story way too much.

Koenig ignored me and went on. "The heirs have produced an inventory list in Mr. Kosta's hand that shows a substantial number of gold coins."

"How many," asked Malika as if the two words were one.

Sarah Koenig straightened her skirt, cleared her throat and said, "The heirs claim there were 271."

When I recovered my wits, I closed my open mouth and pulled out my phone and went for the calculator app. "Let's see what the price of gold is…"

"Don't bother," said Koenig. "270 of the coins were purported to be South African Krugerrands, they'd be worth, over $350,000."

Malika let out a whistle.

"What about number 271," I asked.

Koenig swallowed. "May I have a glass of water?"

"Oh, I'm sorry. Ice?"

"No, just water, please."

Malika had been sitting on the edge of her seat, so was quicker to her feet. In two strides she was in the center of the kitchen, grabbed a glass, filled it, grabbed a coaster, set it on the table. Elapsed time: 16 seconds.

Koenig looked at us both over the top of the glass as she took a sip.

"According to the inventory list, number 271 as you call it, was a $20 gold piece. It's called a Double Eagle. It was designed by the sculptor Augustus Saint-Gaudens in 1933."

Here she paused as if she wanted to make sure she had our attention, and then said, "And it's not supposed to exist."

Sarah Koenig was enjoying telling this story as much as we were hearing it. She eyed us as she took another sip of water.

"In 1933, with the Great Depression and the banking crisis in full swing. President Franklin D. Roosevelt signed Executive Order 6102 which forbade the hoarding of gold coins or gold bullion. There were 445,500, one ounce, 22 karat gold, Double Eagles stamped out that year and sitting in crates at the Denver Mint. Because of EO 6102, 445,498 coins were ordered to be melted down. The gold was to be melted, poured into ingots and stashed at the United States Bullion Depository at Fort Knox. The only two coins that are supposed to exist are in the U.S. National Numismatic Collection at the Smithsonian. But in 2002 there was an auction of a 1933 Double Eagle and an anonymous private buyer paid $7,590,000. If the late Isadore Kosta is to be believed there is at least one more in existence."

We sat in silence a minute before I registered the distress on Sarah Koenig's face.

Finally, she said, "As a matter of form; I take it you haven't come across any gold coins?"

"As a matter of form, no," I said. "There aren't many places to hide things. I didn't have much when I moved in here, but I still....Wait, the golf clubs," I said jumping up from my chair.

"I literally haven't touched this," I said as I reached into the back of my only closet.

Koenig was right at my heels. I hefted the bag. "Well the 270 are not here," I said. My first job ever was as a caddy at Audubon Country Club; muscle memory told me this bag didn't have 270 gold coins. I took all the clubs out anyway and shone a flashlight to the bottom while Koenig unzipped compartments.

"Just your basic rich guy's golf set," I said. "You're welcome to look anywhere. I've got to make a phone call," I said looking at Malika. She nodded and I headed to the aft deck.

I called 911 dispatch. Goldie Skammerhorn's hip had just broken and as she fell, her husband Hubert, at her side for over 70 years, went down with her. Her hip broke and she fell, for him it was the other way around, his hip broke when he hit the floor.

When I came back into the cabin, Malika and Ms. Koenig had just about run out of places to look. I slid the refrigerator out so we could see behind it.

"That leaves the engine compartment," I said as I pushed back the fridge. "And you're not dressed for a crawlspace," I said to Sarah.

"If I could use your bathroom; I brought a change of clothes," she said picking up her handbag.

"Be my guest."

While she changed, I moved the coffee table aside and rolled up the throw-rug the table had been sitting on. As Sarah came out of the bathroom, I was opening the trap door in the floor. She was dressed for gardening: a t-shirt, jean shorts and ratty sneakers.

The engine compartment was barely big enough for two. I got another flash, and suggested Sarah and Malika do the honors. Having been below deck with Crunchy and Bob Shepard, I was confident they were wasting their time.

CHAPTER FORTY-FOUR

Text from Malika: "Number 271"
  Text from Pax: "El Dorado"

When Malika suggested I move in with her, Lt. Natalie Heath was so surprised that she tore her eyes from her spreadsheet. She looked at one then the other of us and then back down to her laptop.

  Malika has a large 150-year-old house on 4th Street in what is referred to as Old Louisville. Originally a single-family home built by a vice-president of the L&N Railroad after the Civil War, the house had already been divided into three apartments when Malika bought it. Hers was probably the smallest unit and on the third floor. The rental income from the other two covered her mortgage with enough left to buy her groceries every month. Her tenants got a bonus of having a police vehicle parked in the drive. Though the van was unmarked, the spray of short antenna on the roof and the narrow row of red and blue lights playing peek-a-boo through the grill didn't fool anyone.

  I was crazy about Malika but preferred we live together on the river. But then I remembered winter was looming. Just the thought of being surrounded by ice-cold water gave me a chill.

  I looked to Malika. "Alright, if Malika will have me, I'll move. But these flashes are coming more frequently. I'm at the center of those circles you've drawn on your map and they keep getting bigger every week. Every now and then, I'm going to have to get out of town just to get a good night's sleep. You're aware the flashes wake me up at night aren't you," I said to Heath.

  She nodded.

  "I have no choice but to play this out to the end, whatever that is."

"What about a sleeping pill," asked Heath.

"My shrink gave me some free samples. I haven't used them. Dr. Newman explained that sleeping pills work on receptors in the brain, so messing with the brain could end all the flashes. We don't know. If I get desperate for sleep, I won't hesitate to try one."

We left the restaurant and since Malika had let the cat out of the bag about our relationship, I embraced her with a long, passionate kiss. In return she gave me a kiss for the kiss.

CHAPTER FORTY-FIVE

Text from Malika: "Brainflash"
Text from Pax: "Brainstorm"

The weather forecast called for evening showers, so I thought this was a good time to move to Malika's place. I went back to Bloomers, to pack a suitcase and a backpack. As soon as I stepped into the cabin, I knew something was amiss. I froze in place and examined every sound for a full minute. Without needing to look, I reached behind me into the corner by the cabin door and put my hand on the knob of my Reggie Jackson model, Louisville Slugger.

The baseball bat had been my father's. In high school he played right field and could bat from either side of the plate. Both of my parents were heavy smokers who never allowed their addiction into the house. Dad kept his Reggie Jackson bat leaning against the house by the back door. At commercial breaks when watching close games on TV, dad would spring from his recliner, step outside and light-up a cigarette. He'd pick up his bat and stand over a particular brick in the patio that had become loose from every time he would tap his bat on 'home plate' before he would swing. We'd hear him mumble encouragement to himself, "Look for a low one on the inside from this guy" and "eye on the ball." Sometimes, I would go out, stand twenty feet in front of him and go into my windup. I would throw that imaginary ball with all my might and at a full count, dad would knock it into the next county.

Back on Bloomers it was time to bring Reggie to the plate. I turned on the lights and looked around for what triggered my suspicion that I'd had an uninvited guest.

It was the throw rug under the coffee-table. I've never been accused of being a neat freak, but there was a dent in one of the wood planks of the floor. I had created the dent by passing out drunk and taking a chair to the floor with me. I hated that mark; it was my scarlet letter. I made sure the rug was always positioned just so, to put that mark out of my sight. Now, my scarlet letter was showing. Someone had moved the coffee table and rug to get into the engine compartment.

I did a thorough top to bottom search of Bloomers but found nothing else out of place or missing.

Malika and I had traded keys the night before. She gave me two keys to her place and from me, she had to settle for a virtual key. I'd never locked the cabin door on the boat and couldn't think where I'd put the set I'd been given. Now I looked a little harder for the keys and found them in the 'junk' drawer in the kitchen where everything that isn't needed much ends up. I put one of the cabin keys on my key ring and would give the other to Malika. She was sure to prefer a real key to the virtual one she got when I explained the door was never locked anyway. The exchange of keys was a sign of trust after all.

The Shepards at one end of the Knights of Columbus dock and Richard Bush at the other end were the only other of my neighbors who lived on their boats full-time. I felt an obligation to let the community know of my suspicion that I'd had an unwanted visitor. This intrusion didn't have the smell of a common thief on the prowl. Nothing was taken and there aren't many thieves who would find easy pickings in an engine compartment. Someone was looking for something and the only something that made sense was 271 gold coins.

After packing my bags, I went to Richard Bush on the Blue Dick to give him the heads up on my unknown visitor.

"Son of a bitch, man," he said. "We've never had any trouble with stealin' down here."

"Well, you still haven't, but someone was on my boat." I told him since the season at Knight's was almost over, I was moving in with my girlfriend for the time being.

"She made you an offer you couldn't refuse, didn't she," he said with a crooked grin.

I allowed only my eyes to smile, "Have we got a date for breakdown yet,"

I said not answering. Every October, the boaters got together to disconnect power lines, drain the water lines and move the Knight's fleet. Some boats are pulled from the water for maintenance and storage, some are even shrink-wrapped. Others are moved to the protection of the marinas for the winter. The winter was too harsh for houseboats and cruisers to weather on these exposed docks.

"No, but you can bet they'll let you know," said Richard.

The Shepards were out so I sat on their deck and wrote them a note which I slid between the pages of a James Lee Burke novel one of them had left on a deck chair. Then I was off to Malika's.

At her house, I used one of the keys she'd given me to open the outer door, but after climbing the steps to her third-floor apartment, I felt a little bit awkward about just walking in. I knocked on her door jamb. The door opened an inch and a single hazel green eye gave me a brief look before the door opened all the way. She wore only a silky, crimson red t-shirt that was enough to cover her. Almost.

In the evening, we decided to investigate the mysterious case of Norman Threadgill. Malika went on-line and pulled up his obituary from the Louisville Courier.

> Norman G. Threadgill
> Louisville—Norman Threadgill, 62, passed away on April 7 at his home. He was born in Ann Arbor, Michigan where he met his wife of 38 years, Althea (Powell) Threadgill. Norman had a B.S. in Geology from the University of Michigan.

Malika stopped reading when I said, "Geology?" I stared up into the ceiling, searching the dark recesses of my mind.

Next to me on the couch, her bare legs creating a nest for her laptop, Malika said, "Right, geology. Ring a bell?"

"Sort of. Not exactly the tools of a geologist, but I'm reminded that Norman left behind two gardening tools."

After waiting about 10 seconds, Malika said, "And?"

"He had no plants. His boat was surrounded by water and the wood planks of a dock. Why did he have gardening tools?"

"Well, the Knights clubhouse probably has flowers."

"He didn't dock at Knights," I said. "He was at River Park Marina at the end of the dock, no flowers, hell, no dirt within 30 yards."

"Still," Malika shrugged her shoulders.

"One of the tools was an auger," I said.

"For making holes?"

"Deep holes. It had a 'T' shaped handle and was probably 4 feet long. You use the handle to screw the auger into the ground, then lift the dirt out of the 3 or 4-inch diameter hole it makes. I gave it to the Goodwill along with the rest of the furniture from my apartment. Right after I bought the boat. I was drinking a lot back then. I guess I didn't give it a second thought."

"How deep a hole would it make?"

It was my turn to shrug my shoulders, "A couple or three feet maybe."

Addressing the same spot on the ceiling I had explored, Malika asked, "So where and why are these holes?"

CHAPTER FORTY-SIX

At 5:15 AM I jerked awake with a flash. Malika, her back pressed against my side woke with a start.

"Sorry, but you might as well get up too. There's been a double homicide."

Malika just listened as I called it in. Then she sighed, kissed me on the cheek, and slipped out of bed. I watched as she walked toward the bathroom pulling the t-shirt over her head as she went. She knew I'd be watching. She turned and fired the balled-up shirt right into my face.

Angela Barton and I had a day of hips and hearts, falls and crashes. And a new one-day record of 19 flashes. Malika had been asked by one of the TV stations to do a live report on the evening news about the double homicide. We arranged to rendezvous at her place before going out to dinner. Louisville Metro police nabbed the dead woman's ex-husband as he was about to depart from his east-end apartment in his RV. Because I was able to identify the shooter, two LMPD officers were hiding in the bushes of the guy's apartment by the time he returned home from his killing spree.

To explain the quick arrest, Malika told the press, what most of them already knew from watching TV police dramas, the ex-spouse is automatically the prime suspect in such cases. Seeking verisimilitude, 911 dispatch sent police officers to the homes of both ex-spouses of the murdered couple.

At dinner, Malika told me the killer, Jason Stills, had been all set to vanish. He had counterfeit identity papers, $150,000 in cash and the RV was topped off with 150 gallons of gas. All he had left to do was to hook his compact car to the tow bar and be gone. When the cops jumped out of the bushes, Stills lost control of his bladder and the gun fell from his waistband. She'd watched the arrest from the cop's body cameras. A by-the-book take down. And she was sure the videos would be used in training programs because who doesn't want to see a bad guy jump out of his skin as a dark stain blossoms on his khakis?

The 271 gold coins were never far from my mind. It occurred to me that besides some dirty underwear, the French postcards were the only thing Mr. Threadgill left behind that were of a truly personal nature. I decided the postcard collection needed more than just my prurient scrutiny. When I'd packed to come to Malika's, I'd tossed the Tupperware container with the cards into my suitcase.

After dinner, Malika and I sat side by side on her couch and discussed the Threadgill case. We came up with a plan. I would go to Google Translate in order to read the messages on the postcards and she would look up the coroner's report to find the cause of death. As the police P.I.O. Malika had ready access to such things. We turned on our lap-top computers.

CARTE POSTALE
Mademoiselle Marguerite Laudry
Maison Beaujolais

Somehow, I knew that maison meant house. So, instead of a street address, it looks like in 1903, houses in the city of Tours, had names. The message that was written was more difficult because less care was taken with the cursive penmanship. I made out the words, bonne sante et Bonheur and entered them into the computer. I determined that Mademoiselle Laudry who lived in the Beaujolais House was receiving wishes for good health and happiness. The woman on the picture side of the card wearing only her bloomers looked healthy enough but seemed to be lacking something in the happiness department.

The cursive writing on the cards was very unlike my own handwriting. The letters were calligraphy in their beauty. They weren't necessarily legible, but they were beautiful. I paged through the stack of the two dozen or so cards I had. About half-way through was a card where the writing was straight as if written on invisible lines, the letters easily identified. Some of these words looked familiar. The card read, "Trente-huit trois sept deux quatre quatre deux. Quatre-vingt-cinq six trois trois zero trois huit."

"Hey," I said, "look at this."

The card was addressed to a Mademoiselle Nelly and I was sure I'd seen the same address on another card. I skipped the first word, which was Bonjour, and typed in: trente-huit. I hit 'Enter'.

The translation read "38."

I typed in the rest and got, "372442 85633038."

"What is that," Malika said.

"No idea."

We compared the postcards. Not all were used cards. Some were merely old blank cards that had never been mailed. The ones that were used had French stamps with a cost of "10c." 10 centimes as it turned out. But the stamp on the Nelly card read "10 Cents." This stamp, though similar in design, was a U.S. stamp and below the picture of a dour looking man in tiny print was the name "Webster." Daniel Webster, I decided. This stamp was not cancelled.

Malika, sitting next to me on the couch, picked up my computer which was still in the Google Translate mode and finished inputting the message. The un-signed card ended with a very un-French, "bonne journee," better known to Americans everywhere as "Have a nice day."

"Merde," I said. "Pardon my French."

CHAPTER FORTY-SEVEN

Text from Malika: "38372442"

Text from me: "Pardon My French"

Angela and I were on a run to an injury accident in the Highview area. She was behind the wheel as we passed a strip mall. I caught the name of one of the shops, The 38th Parallel. I liked the name. Something about the design of the sign left me with the impression the store sold hiking and adventure gear. It was hours later when Angela and I had stopped for a junk-food dinner, that I recalled the first two words I translated from the postcard were 'thirty-eight.' Pulling out my phone I touched the Google microphone symbol and said: "what are the co-ordinates of Louisville, KY."

Instantly, the answer came back: 38.2527 N, 85.7585 W.

Malika was on a co-ed volleyball team that was playing that night in the sand, under the lights. I sent her a text to call me when she had time. I was walking back to the ambulance when my phone rang.

"Hey, what's up Pax-man?"

"Pax-man? Really?"

"Sorry, I just had a perfect set-up shot that Tina spiked to win the game; I'm a little fired-up here."

"I want to be there," I said.

"Good, because I put you on the waiting list. You're number one, as soon as a guy drops out, you're in."

"Great. Hey, the numbers on the postcard, the first set started with 38, do you remember any numbers from the second set?"

"Let's see. One of the sets had a lot of threes, and the second set started with an eight," Malika said.

I didn't speak.

"Hello," she said.

"Sorry, I was just thinking. If that second set starts with an eight-five, then I think these numbers are the co-ordinates to somewhere right in this area."

"That would fit," Malika said.

"Yeah, I remember a grade school assignment," I said, "Louisville shares the 38th parallel with Wichita, Kansas; Athens, Greece and Seoul, South Korea. But I remember only one city on the 85 degrees longitude."

"Would that be Louisville?"

"It would."

I didn't get home until 3 AM. I took off my shoes outside the apartment door to enter as quietly as I could. It was a wasted effort. Taped to the bedroom door was a sheet of paper, in bold Sharpie were the words, "WAKE ME." Malika was in bed, on her back, her mouth was open just a little. She was sound asleep. I watched her with envy for a minute and thought about ignoring her note. I could sleep on the couch but for the bold print on the note. I tip-toed in, leaned over and kissed her on the cheek.

"Hey there," I whispered.

She stirred a little and smiled. I delivered a couple more kisses and she opened her eyes a smidge.

"Hey, you're home," she said.

"I'm waking you against my better judgement."

Her eyes came open all the way, "Oh, yeah," she said swinging her feet out of bed.

Not stopping for a robe or slippers, she took my hand and pulled me into the kitchen where her laptop was open on the kitchen table.

"I entered all the numbers on Google Maps, but I couldn't bring myself to press the 'Enter' button without you here," Malika said.

"Wow, what restraint."

"You should do the honors," she said moving the mouse to bring the screen to life.

I sat down in front of the computer and pulled her to my lap. Reaching around her, I paused over the keyboard.

I checked the two sets of eight-digit numbers Malika had put in the search box.

"Crunchy and I have done some Geocaching where we entered co-ordinates on his app. I think we need to put a period after the first two digits of each set."

That done, "The postcard doesn't say, but we'll assume the first set of digits is latitude. Around Louisville, that would be north latitude, so we'll put an N after that set. The second set is longitude and in this part of the world that would be west," I said as I plugged in a 'W' at the end of the row of numbers.

"Ok, ready? Here we go," I said, as I hit "Enter." On the screen we soared from our invisible spacecraft around planet earth. We descended into the United States, flew low into the Ohio Valley and landed on a small island in the Ohio River called Embry.

"Where the hell is that," I said.

CHAPTER FORTY-EIGHT

Backing up again, a little higher into space, we could see that Embry Island was located halfway between Six Mile Island and Eighteen Mile Island. Neither of us had ever heard of this other name for Twelve Mile Island. The names Six, Twelve and Eighteen Mile were perfect because they represented a distance and location at the same time. The numbers told how far each island was from downtown Louisville.

Our next move back on terra firma would be a trip to Twelve Mile. The wait for that adventure would be excruciating. Malika and I both had responsible jobs and were damned to the end of our days to be responsible people. We couldn't just bring ourselves to call in sick. Malika's second in command was on maternity leave; I couldn't just leave Angela when heavy rains and therefore many accidents, were forecast. Besides, maybe the geologist in Threadgill, assuming he had written the postcard at all, had discovered an interesting fossil. Tourists traveled to the Falls of the Ohio from all over the globe to gaze on the oldest fossil bed in the world and it lay only twelve miles to the west of these postcard coordinates. We resolved to sit tight, plan, wait for our moment and keep our mouths shut.

The next evening a police officer was shot. LMPD Patrol officer Katherine Eickmann, responding to a 911 "break-in in progress," was hit in the shoulder as she was about to step from her patrol car. She managed, in a weak voice, to utter two words before she passed out, "officer down."

Gene Woods was sitting on his back porch, two blocks from the shooting, smoking his last cigarette of the day and sipping his nightly, "medicinal" bourbon when it dawned on him the sirens he was hearing were getting louder. He couldn't determine which direction the sound was coming from because they were coming from everywhere. Every LMPD officer whether on duty or off, every Jefferson County Sheriff's Deputy, every FBI and DEA officer in the city, converged on that neighborhood from every direction. Code 3. With lights flashing and sirens screaming, police helicopters blinding the area with powerful searchlights, Mr. Woods thought the world was coming to an end.

EMS unit 147 with EMT Charlie Altman and Paramedic John Cobbs was the first of three EMS teams to arrive. They stopped the bleeding, started an IV and rushed Eickmann to Moore High School, just two blocks away, where a STAT Flight helicopter had just touched down and was ready to transport her to University Hospital. The trauma team was prepped and waiting when her gurney was pushed into the operating room. It was quickly evident to the surgeon that Officer Eickmann was hit with a hollow point bullet designed to expand when it hit hard tissue like bone. Six inches to the left and the round would have gone through the windshield, instead of the open door.

Through the window and the bullet would have been in the expanded stage when it hit her shoulder and would have done so much soft tissue damage, she would have bled out before anyone could reach her. Eickmann's shoulder was lost, but her life was saved. At 31, her career as a police officer was over.

The blue digits on the clock read 2:14 when Malika came home. She fell into bed exhausted and fully clothed. She was barely awake as I took off her shoes and uniform and kissed the dry tracks on her cheeks left behind by a stream of tears.

The next morning as we were replenishing the inventory on our ambulance at the start of our shift, a call came over the intercom telling Angela and me to report to the director's office. Brenda Trainor didn't hear my knock but through the window in her door, we could see her gray mop of hair above the two computer monitors on her desk. Angela opened the door.

"You wanted to see us Director," Angela said, dropping the usual informality.

"Have a seat," Trainor said as she came from behind her desk to join us in the cluster of chairs circling a coffee table in the front area of her office. "I've been on the horn with the police chief this morning, we want to post you two to the Highview neighborhood today."

"Ok," we said as one.

"Not so fast, let me give you all the facts," Trainor said. "Lt. Heath checked her maps and spreadsheet last night, and reported that if you'd been at central dispatch or the house you're living in; on 4th Street is it?"

"Yes ma'am," I said.

"You still would have been out of range of this shooting," Trainor finished.

I raised my voice in anger, "And even if I had been in range, she still would have been shot. I couldn't have stopped that, I can't **predict** anything, you know."

I hadn't slept well and was, in fact, awake when Malika had stumbled into bed at 2:14 AM because of four flashes I'd had between 11 PM and 2:00 AM. Three flashes were over-doses (one died) and the fourth was a drunk who'd cracked his head when he fell off his perch from atop a chair as he stretched to peek through a neighbor's window.

Angela touched my arm and turned on that soft, café au lait voice, "We know you can't make predictions Paxton. She wasn't suggesting this was your fault. But if Officer Eickmann hadn't been able to call after she was shot, we'd be going to her funeral."

I turned to Brenda Trainor and bowed slightly, "Sorry, not sleeping well."

Trainor shook it off and said, "No worries, Pax." Indeed, she continued as if my little outburst hadn't taken place. "The 9-1-1 call that sent Kathy Eickmann into harm's way, was bogus. The call was not traceable; probably from a disposal phone. CSI thinks the shot was fired from a tree; would you believe. Like a hunter out in the country in a tree stand. The cops think she was lured into a trap so she could be shot. We don't have a motive. We don't know if the shooter has a beef with cops, first-responders or Eickmann in particular. There will be a lot of patrol cars in the area, both marked and unmarked. You won't be alone, but you could be a target. We just don't know."

Director Trainor paused and then looked at me directly. "We need Vulcan out there, one way or another. If you're uncomfortable, being exposed, driving around in the truck, just say so and we'll put you in the target area, inside Moore High School."

I looked at my partner. It only took a glance. Her teeth were clenched, her brown eyes, steely and unblinking, she didn't need to say a word.

"We'll stay in our truck," I said. "We'll want to be a visible presence on the streets."

"Alright. I'm changing your shift so you're on duty until midnight. Go home, rest up and start fresh at 2PM." With that, the director stood, giving us our cue that the meeting was over. Brenda Trainor looked at each of us individually and said," I've got two conditions. You **will** wear bullet-proof vests and you **will** drive the streets for your whole shift. No parking the unit like sitting ducks between runs. Got it?"

Again, we answered in unison, "Yes, ma'am."

Trainor opened the office door for us and said, "I'll see that your vests are in the supply room at the start of your shift. Thank you both."

CHAPTER FORTY-NINE

I knew Malika would be busy, so I sent her a text message letting her know of my shift change and area assignment. She called just as I was getting into bed.

"Hey, thanks for putting me to bed the other night."

"Anytime you need help removing your clothes, I'm your man," I said.

She snorted but then turned serious. "I hear you and Angela should be getting hazardous duty pay."

"Funny, that's something the Director didn't mention," I said. "I guess it should have occurred to me the police public information officer would know all about my new assignment."

"That's because this P.I.O. is interested in all things Paxton Gahl. I couldn't come up with a viable argument for keeping you out of the Highview area. By the same token, there was no argument for you not to have a bulletproof vest."

"That was your idea?" I asked.

"Yes, which reminds me, do you have Angela's cell number?"

I gave Malika the number. "What's this about," I asked.

"Just some girl talk. None of your business," she said, dismissing my question. "I'll be awake until you're home, safe and sound, so don't go out partying after your shift."

It was my turn to snort.

Malika's discretion was thwarted five minutes into our shift.

"Man, your girlfriend saved you from having to work with a cranky partner today," Angela said.

"Thank god for that. What did she do?"

"She advised me not to wear a bra under this Kevlar vest. These things are snug, and I would have been trussed up like Queen Victoria."

"That would be bad," I agreed.

Tuesday's shift from 2PM to midnight exhausted both Angela and me. Our route was confined to the Highview area without many calls, but the tension of wondering if someone was searching for us in the crosshairs of a rifle did us in. Two cars were sent on every police run. Every EMS run got police backup. We lasted longer on Wednesday going from 2PM to Thursday morning at 6AM, but we were exhausted and should have stopped at 5. Angela crashed on the station's couch as soon as we got out of the truck.

I went directly to the radiology department at the cancer center, hoping they could fit me in early. They made me their first patient of the day. I lay still on the platform for a brief blast of radiation into my cheek and was asleep in an instant. When I awoke, the green, mesh mask across my face was still fastened to the table and I wondered if they were done. The rapid faux click of keys directed my eyes to my left where a radiation therapist sat in a chair next to me holding her phone. "Maureen," according to her name tag, put away her phone when my hand moved, as reflex, when I woke to find something covering my face. As she unfastened the mask, she said, "I could have given you another five minutes."

"For what?" I said as it occurred to me that the chair she was sitting in hadn't been there when I laid down.

"You've been asleep for twenty-eight minutes. I've never seen anybody fall asleep so fast. That had to be a record." Her voice turned more somber, "I know you guys have been hitting it pretty hard. I didn't see the point in waking you before I needed to."

"I appreciate that. I'm fine," said Mr. Macho, swinging my feet off the table before I remembered the whole table I was on had been raised up to the business end of the radiation machine. Coming down off that table was like hitting the last step on a staircase before realizing it is six inches deeper than the other stairs. Maureen had seen this mistake before and caught me before I nosed-dived into the floor.

On my way home from radiation, I realized two things: My internal auto-pilot had to be disabled because it was steering me to Bloomers and not to Malika's and after making that correction, I recalled that the next day, Friday, was a radiation and chemotherapy day. It made me a little uncomfortable to realize I was looking forward to getting a sedative as I lay in a heated recliner under a pre-warmed blanket. In the two previous chemo sessions, with the IV in my arm, I'd had the most deeply restful sleep, and no flashes.

If not for being on the edge of our seats for most of the night, our shift was unremarkable. On the following Monday, at the regular meeting of the Vulcan club, I would learn that the neighborhood had about half the number of EMS calls that experience would have predicted. The numbers would crawl back up over the next three days until the area was again meeting the predicted numbers of auto accidents, broken hips and heart attacks. But, for a while, people were behaving themselves.

Friday morning, I had my last radiation treatment. The end was marked by a ceremonial bell ringing in the waiting room. To a round of applause, I was presented with a very colorful, Certificate of Accomplishment signed by the staff. Somehow, this whole event seemed backward since all I did was show up and lie down. I was a bit embarrassed as I thanked them all. I refrained from telling them I hoped never to see them again, since they must have heard that many times.

My last chemo was at noon the same day, which I hoped would be a rest period before my shift started at 2PM. Dr. Newman was waiting for me when I arrived, as usual, and this time, lying in my heated recliner, I was able to describe a flash as it was happening. I pulled out my phone and punched the number.

"What's up Vulcan," was the answer on the other end. All the dispatchers knew my name was Paxton by this time, but they all preferred Vulcan.

"A kid named Barbara Kaminer, broken ankle, on the Water Tower at Zorn and River Road. They may need a hook and ladder to get her down, she's on top of the portico that goes around the base of the tower. I think that's about 25 or 30 feet off the ground."

"Got it, thanks."

The nurse had already hooked up the IV and the sedative was kicking in. I closed my eyes and told Dr. Newman, "the only information 9-1-1 needs is what I just gave. But. Two other kids were involved."

Because flashes were coming in around the clock, I was more tired than ever, and the sedative had less work to do. "Lon and Josh, I struggled with the last name Kam-in, Kamn, Kam In Err, are her two big brothers. They're with her. Probably put her up to it."

"How did they get up there," said Newman. "I know where you're talking about. I don't see how they could get up there."

"Don't know," I said.

"Do you get a picture of the place?"

I opened my eyes a fraction. "Yes.... But I know the place anyway. Beautiful. Went to a wedding there." Then I started to laugh as the little gray cells connected the dots, "Hey, that was my wedding."

CHAPTER FIFTY

After two nights patrolling in the Highview neighborhood and flashes occurring around the clock, I needed to get out of Dodge and away from people. When I awoke from the longest break between flashes, one hour and forty-five minutes, it was Saturday morning.

Malika greeted me with a big hug and kiss when I walked into the kitchen. She said, "I have a surprise for you."

I managed to raise my eyebrows a few millimeters.

"We're taking a trip," she said.

"When?"

"Right now."

"Can I have breakfast first?"

Malika turned around and pulled from the oven an aluminum foil wrapped package. She bent back one corner and held it to my nose. An egg, bacon and cheese sandwich.

"Marry me," I said automatically.

The startled look on her face must have matched the one on mine.

"Who said that," I said, looking around the room.

"I'm going to let that one slide," she said. "You're not yourself."

"Well, I ahh,...."

"Not another word," Malika said, first putting a finger to my lips, and then pressing her lips to mine. She thrust her tongue between my lips and as my hands began to wander from her hips, she grabbed them. "No, no, we have to leave right now. The van is packed, coffee is in the thermos. If you want to grab something, grab your sandwich and the fresh squeezed O.J. in the fridge. I'm driving."

Malika took us east out the two lanes of River Road with its gentle, languid curves that mimicked the flow of the Ohio running beside it. Thirty minutes later we pulled into the immense and empty parking lot of a popular restaurant not open on a Saturday morning. My breakfast consumed, I carried the thermos and followed Malika, with a peacock blue nylon bag over one shoulder.

The restaurant, Captain's Quarters, is strategically situated at the mouth of Harrods Creek where it feeds the Ohio. To encourage the boating crowd, CQ has a docking area for boating customers. The only boat parked there on this sunny morning, was Bloomers.

At the flying bridge under the Bimini top was Cliff and in a wide brimmed red hat was his squeeze, Teresa. Malika turned and in a tentative voice said, "Surprise."

Malika was aware Cliff knew about my flashes. She called him and said that I needed to get out of town, away from a large population of people, who do things like have accidents, heart attacks, and shoot each other. She suggested to Cliff that a boat trip to Twelve Mile Island would be just the thing. Unbeknownst to him she had rented a metal detector from a hardware store and stashed it along with a shovel on-board Bloomers.

After greetings and hugs all round, I took the wheel and piloted us out onto the river. Teresa and Cliff went back up to the top deck and Malika stood by my side to bring me up to speed. Malika hadn't told Cliff that we thought there might be a fortune in gold buried on the island.

"Your postcards, your friend, your call," she said. "If you want to just keep it between you and me, we can just hang-out on the island and relax."

I smiled, "No, Cliff is good people. And he trusts Teresa. This is a good idea M, thanks."

As if she'd been under water, Malika let out a big breath of air, "Oh, thank god. I thought I would burst."

We had a three-mile voyage from the Harrod's Creek dock, so Malika and I worked out our plan. Twelve Mile Island was a popular destination for boaters and the forecast was for a cloudy, but rain-free weekend in the mid-70s. Unlike Six Mile Island which hugged the Indiana shore and Eighteen Mile Island which hugged the Kentucky shore, Twelve Mile was in the center of a wide section of the Ohio. A swimmer risking life and limb among the boats would have to fight, at least a quarter of a mile of swift current to reach the island.

We could expect plenty of people on the island which is over a mile long and shaped like a marquise diamond. It is almost a quarter of a mile wide in the middle. The satellite photo of the island we'd looked at on that early morning when we punched in the co-ordinates, showed a small harbor and a long staircase on the eastern end of the island that faced Kentucky. We would look for a cove on the western end away from the crowd that was sure to come on a day like this.

After snuggling into a cove that fit Bloomers like a glove, we tied off and asked Teresa and Cliff to join us inside. Since my surgery, radiation and chemo, I quit ignoring the fact that the sun not only provides Vitamin D, it will also supply melanoma given the chance. I hated smearing on sunscreen but did it anyway.

In my 'living room,' I began.

"What I'm about to tell you, was learned by Malika and me, after we signed a confidentiality agreement. So, consider yourself signed up too."

"If this is about the flashes, Cliff told me all about that. I'll never tell, I'm in the jewelry business, when you have slimy customers who have both wives and girl-friends, you learn to keep a secret." said Teresa.

"No, it's not about that. It's about this boat and these," I said handing her the postcards.

When I finished telling the whole story, Teresa could only say "Wow," and stare first at Malika, then me. Cliff got up without a word, walked three spaces to the closet and pulled out a plastic case the size of a large briefcase.

"I brought this to use as a toy this weekend, but it's just become a tool," he said. "Let's do a little recon."

He opened the case and I saw it was the drone Crunchy and Teresa's boys were assembling when they had me over for dinner a couple of months ago. I smacked my forehead, "I forgot to ask about the boys. Do you have them stashed in the hold?"

"Liam and Noah are with their dad this weekend," said Teresa, "this isn't just a get-a-way for you, ya' know."

Cliff's drone controller had two joy sticks and a small video monitor. Malika handed Cliff the co-ordinates she had written on an index card and he entered the numbers. Teresa carried the drone and led the way up the ladder to the upper deck. She set the drone on a supply chest holding life preservers and folding chairs.

"This little thing is a camera," Cliff said pointing to a small lens. "We'll have a live, bird's eye view here," he said, pointing to the 7 x 5-inch screen. We huddled in close. Everyone was glad I'd taken a shower that morning.

When it took off, the drone sounded like a thousand angry bees. The site was only about 200 yards away and the drone arrived in minutes. The spot was un-remarkable. Trees and foliage were fairly dense as this, the western end of the island, doesn't get the visitors like the eastern end does.

Cliff brought the drone down to about ten feet in a clearing among forty-foot sycamores. He had it slowly rotate 360 degrees as we looked for any signs digging in the area. Nothing was obvious.

Before returning the drone to its "hangar," Cliff sent the drone over the whole end of the island looking to see if there might any visitors heading our way. Seeing nothing, he signaled the 'all clear,' and summoned the drone back to Bloomers. We picked up our gear and disembarked from Bloomers. With a shovel slung over my shoulder, I pulled up the Geocaching app on my phone and led the way.

After a walk of five minutes, I called a halt to the expedition. "This is it." I indicated the spot with my toe.

Malika was up next. She had rented the metal detector and the guy at the hardware store had shown her how it worked. She turned it on and began swinging the dinner plate sized wand over the ground. After thirty seconds, she got a beep. It was my turn now and I brought my spade to the spot.

Teresa said, "Wait." She pulled her cell phone from her pocket. She would document our search from the moment when I dug-up the first of several beer bottle caps. Malika kept widening her circle of search. I handed Cliff the phone and he walked into the woods and came at the same coordinates from a different direction. This time when he said, "This is it," he was ten feet from the first spot. Twice more he walked into the woods and came at it from a different direction marking each attempt with an "X" made with his boot-heel.

I looked at the four spots, estimated an average and said, "Malika, try here."

She moved across the ground slowly, swinging the disc parallel to the earth, inches above. Silence. Her search area expanded to five square feet, and then ten. "Beep, beep, beep, beep." The sound was insistent and louder than before.

I was poised with a shovel over the spot until Teresa was ready with the camera and said, "Action." I drove the shovel to the hilt, the earth softer than before. I cleared a hole a foot in diameter, expecting something big like a beer can, but seeing nothing. Malika put the disc of the detector in the hole and got....nothing.

I kicked around the dirt I had removed with the shovel, thinking I must have dug it up, whatever "it" was. Again, nothing.

Cliff said to Malika, "Try putting the detector in the hole first and then turn it on."

When frantic beeping resumed, we all looked at Cliff who just shrugged his shoulders and said, "Don't ask me."

I expanded the diameter of the hole and went deeper until the shovel rang out a metallic "clink".

The tube we uncovered was free of rust, about an inch and a half in diameter and two and a half feet long. And it was heavy. From the moment we pulled it out, there wasn't much doubt as to what was inside. The steel tube and its contents would weigh in at 20 pounds, about the same as 2 ½ gallons of milk. The top and bottom had screw off caps which were sealed in a hard, brick red wax. Teresa, our resident jeweler, recognized the wax. "In olden times," she said, forgetting she wasn't talking to her kids, "they would melt the end of a stick of wax like this with a candle, let it drip on the flap edge of an envelope and press their signet ring with the family crest into the molten wax." Then, remembering her audience, she blushed and added, "I think the seal will be tough to break."

Teresa was right about that. Back on Bloomers I was a little short on tools, so I went to Threadgill's golf bag. My club selection was a putter. Tapping away at one end broke off some wax but the cap wouldn't budge. After debating the merits of using a flame on the cap to loosen the wax that had flowed into the threads, we decided to try it.

On the forward deck, Malika wielded a rolled-up magazine as a torch, Cliff held one end of the cylinder and Teresa filmed. I was ready with a towel and oven mitt and when the first drop of wax hit the paper towel Malika had positioned on the deck, I grabbed hold of the cap and twisted. The cap turned very slowly—to a point. After repeating the procedure twice more, the cap came off entirely.

Cliff carried the tube back inside the cabin. He held it vertically on the coffee table. Teresa had not stopped documenting the event with her phone. We all peered into the tube to see a frilly material of emerald green. I looked at my three friends. No one spoke. Milking the event for all it was worth, I played the part of magician. I took a pinch of material, paused for effect and voila.

Cliff poured out the coins in a smooth row. The air that was sucked out of the room by the collective intake of breath made my ears pop. We all stared in silence and wonder at all that gleaming gold. Without regard to the value, I was in awe of the rich color, the beauty and weight of the coins.

After a moment of silence, Malika started stacking the coins in columns of tens. I joined her and when we finished, we counted exactly twenty-seven stacks. 270 South African Krugerrands. But there was no 1933 Double Eagle. Cliff held up the frilly green material which was, of course, a pair of lady's bloomers. We stared at the gold for a while longer and then loaded the Krugerrands back into the tube. We stashed the pipe in the engine room where the steel tube blended into its environment. We resumed our holiday weekend as if nothing extraordinary had happened. NOT!

By Sunday, I was refreshed, and Malika and I were getting used to nights of uninterrupted sleep. She suggested I ease back into the grind, so on Sunday afternoon we cruised back to Harrods Creek and dropped Teresa and Cliff at Captain's Quarters. Malika and I returned to K of C and she spent a rest-full night. I texted in to 911 three flashes, but two others were more urgent, a stabbing and a heart attack, and I left our bed to call those in.

CHAPTER FIFTY-ONE

Maybe Malika, Teresa, Cliff and I probably all had the same thought, 'What would it be like if we keep the gold? Who would ever know?' I admit I had that thought. Finders, keepers? None of us ever said it out loud. $87,500 each. Those were numbers that could change lives.

I called Sarah Koenig on her cell at 9AM Monday morning. "Can you meet me at the bank at 10?"

"Sure, what's this about?"

"See you at 10," I said as I hung up.

Malika had gone to her apartment to change and was waiting for me in the Origins Bank parking lot when I arrived. An upstanding officer of the law was my witness of the entire adventure of exploration, discovery and the return of the loot. Ms. Koenig and the acting president of Origins were waiting for us when we walked in together. I carried the steel pipe in one hand. In an inner office, I poured the coins onto a desk and put an end to their smiles when I said, "It's not there." They knew I was referring to the Double Eagle.

The 270 Krugerrands would match Isadore Kosta's inventory list of his safety deposit contents. The bank could still claim there was no proof the Double Eagle ever existed, but their case was considerably weakened.

I handed Ms. Koenig the Bloomers postcards and told them I would wait while they made photocopies and gave me a signed receipt for the gold. Malika got Koenig's email address and called Teresa. Teresa forwarded the video she had made of the search and discovery.

Leaving the bank, I leaned down to give Malika a 'see you later' kiss. She grabbed a hand-full of my shirt and pulled me in for a smooch that warmed me with pleasure. When my eyes uncrossed, I said, "Tell me what I did, and I'll do it again."

"It's what you didn't do. You never suggested we should just keep the gold."

Getting in my car, I tossed the postcards, in a clear plastic envelope, onto the seat beside me. A half-naked woman in bloomers looked up at me. When I reached to turn it over, I remembered turning over the framed postcard on the wall in the cabin aboard Bloomers the day the Malika came to visit me for the first time. I had forgotten to bring along that particular postcard for Koenig tor copy. A task for another day. When I returned to Bloomers to collect my dirty laundry, I tossed the framed card in the hamper too. One of the amenities at Malika's house was a washer and dryer in the basement.

Driving to Malika's, I pulled over to read a text from Brenda Trainor. "See me before your shift," it read.

As expected, I had been re-assigned to work in the dispatch office.

I walked Angela to her ambulance where she would wait for her new partner. "Who are you getting," I asked.

"Some rookie named Lee Erwin," she said.

I held out my hand and said, "Don't be too hard on him or her."

Angela looked briefly at my outstretched hand, slapped it away and gave me a big hug. "Take care of yourself Paxton."

"Stay in touch Angela."

CHAPTER FIFTY-TWO

The Emergency Communications System for Louisville is in a fortress that used to house the Federal Reserve Bank. There is a guard house overlooking the street where armored cars loaded with newly printed greenbacks pulled into the enclosed loading bay to deliver their millions. It was where beat-up old cash went to die, where bales of money were burned. When air pollution became an issue, the old money was shredded instead. Bits of shredded cash can still be seen in hard to reach crevices of the shred room. Steel bank vault doors, three feet thick now stand permanently open in the basement.

The communications center is on the third floor in a large room perhaps 500 feet square. The room is dimly lit to make it easier to view the hundred or so monitors and seating for about 20 dispatchers. For training I sat behind Nancy Goldstein looking over her shoulder. Looking over Nancy's shoulder is not difficult whether she is standing or sitting since she barely reached 5 feet in heels. Nancy was answering 911 calls and dispatching emergency help. I was getting flashes with some frequency and I would sit behind her, tell her about the flashes, and she would explain why she chose which unit to send in response. Nancy had spent five years on the tier one level of the dispatch office and now was on tier two. Tier one folks are the big sieve, they get all the calls, most of which are not emergencies.

"9-1-1, what is your emergency?"

"My brother hit me, and my mother said to call 9-1-1."

Or

"Dominos delivered the wrong pizza."

Since all my flashes were actual emergencies, I worked with Nancy on tier two as she took calls filtered by the tier one group. Nancy sent police, fire or EMS and sometimes all three to the same scene. I watched Nancy work for a few hours and fed her so many flashes, that the other dispatchers were idled. They would come over and watch the spectacle of me now, very tired, lying on the floor of the dimly lit room, Nancy's sweater as a pillow.

By day three of my training, I was sitting next to Nancy at a monitor wearing a headset with a microphone. Brad Wilhoit, one of the other tier two dispatchers in the next booth said, "Hey Vulcan, you missed one."

I was surprised, "What? What'd I miss?"

"Shooting, two hit, Audubon Park area, near that railroad trestle over Preston Street."

"No kidding." I knew without looking at the map, the area was well within my range. Then I got a flash of 71-year-old Stephanie Jenkins falling down her basement steps with a concussion. She lived a half mile further than Audubon Park.

I hit the foot pedal that was my mic switch. "All units be advised—Reason to believe Audubon shooting call is bogus. Repeating—Audubon shooting may be bogus." I didn't need to elaborate for the cops, they knew Patrol Officer Eickmann was blindsided by the trap of a bogus 9-1-1 call. I frantically gestured to Nancy to step in, then I rolled my chair back out of the way to watch a pro in action.

I listened as she repeated my instructions in a calmer, intelligible voice. She directed the police helicopter on airborne patrol, to the scene. Goldstein enlarged the area on the map of her largest computer monitor and we watched the GPS highlight dots of police cars converge toward the train trestle.

"Unit 41 take your next left, go two blocks and turn right on Robin Road.

"Unit 82 take Fayette Avenue to Hart. Unit 114 continue down Preston, lights and siren, but slow like you're searching. If he's on the trestle, he can probably see you. The rest of you, cut your sirens and approach on foot when you're a block away. Eyes in the trees."

Since the Eickmann shooting, officers were reminded daily to look up in trees and buildings, because the crime techs had indeed determined the shot fired into her had come from a tree roost. All officers knew this, but in the heat of the hunt, they had the calm steady voice of a pro like Nancy Goldstein in their ear to remind them.

Then we waited.

Finally, we heard from Patrolman Stanley Glass, "I have eyes on a man with a rifle atop the railroad trestle."

"Unit 114, pull off of the street immediately, we don't need a decoy anymore." If the sniper, Bob Ederle by name, had been paying attention, he would have noticed the flow of traffic beneath him had been pinched off. Road blocks had been set up in both directions on Preston.

From a police helicopter we heard, "All units, be advised, north bound train approaching the trestle, ETA is one minute."

Dispatcher Brad Wilhoit in the next chair said, "Should I call the railroad?"

"No time, but try anyway," said Nancy.

Silent footage from police body camera would show Ederle's grisly end. He was surrounded by officers on each end of the trestle and both sides of the track. In the film, officers on the south end pointed to the coming train. Ederle dropping his rifle, starting one way then the other. When he decided to run north, away from the coming train, he took two steps and then fell. The engineer on the train had started braking and blowing his horn as soon as he saw the police officers with their guns drawn but the locomotives would be 50 yards beyond the trestle before he was able to bring the mile-long line of cars behind him to a halt.

In the dispatch office as we waited for word, I said, "Lights out."

Ballistics would show that Ederle's rifle was the one used to shoot Officer Eickmann. No motive was ever discovered.

I sat back in my chair happy to relax after twenty, very intense minutes. Brad Wilhoit walked over from his station to give me a high five, "Way to go man."

I looked at him, smiled and then bolted upright. "Shit, Stephanie Jenkins, I forgot about Stephanie Jenkins."

"Relax, relax," said Wilhoit holding up both hands in the international gesture of stop, "we got that one the old-fashioned way. Her daughter was in the house and called it in. EMS is there. She'll be fine." I realized Wilhoit threw in that last part for my benefit. He didn't know her condition. Dispatchers usually do not hear the outcomes of the emergency calls they answer.

CHAPTER FIFTY-THREE

The next week was one of the worst of my life. I was getting flashes around the clock because the area the flashes were coming from continued to expand. I told Malika I thought I could make it till Wednesday before I had to get out of town to rest. On Monday, my neighbor, Richard Bush called to tell me someone had broken into my boat. On Tuesday, I was shot.

"I just came back from, the aaa.., grocery," I think he hesitated with the word grocery because he was searching for a synonym for liquor store, "and noticed the door of your cabin swinging open and shut in the chop," Richard said. "I looked through the windows, but didn't go in. The place is a wreck. You want me to call the cops?"

"I'll do that Richard, thanks for calling." In the dispatch office, I sent a patrol car to the scene. Nancy Goldstein was in the chair next to me and gave me permission to check on my home.

I called Malika on the way to my car. She was at the scene of Louisville's 100th homicide of the year, out of Vulcan range on the south-western fringe of Jefferson County. Every news outlet would be highlighting this infamous milestone, so she couldn't get away.

Pulling into the Knights parking lot, I was a little embarrassed to see, not one, but three police cars. Besides the one I had sent, Lt. Heath was there and she'd brought along a crime scene tech named Danny George.

I stopped to talk with an LMPD officer who was coming up the steps I was going down, as I went to the dock. The shiny brass plate on her uniform blouse read, "Officer J. Alvarez." I was in my EMS uniform and introduced myself. "You must be here about my boat, I'm Paxton Gahl."

"Jessica Alvarez," she said shaking my hand. "Lt. Heath just arrived. You're in good hands. I've got to help with a pickup truck that lost its load of cardboard on I-71. Good luck," she said, hurrying off.

Only two things remained on the boat that I cared about. The Reggie Jackson Louisville Slugger that had been my father's and the stack of 33 1/3 LP albums that had been my mother's. I kept the albums for sentimental reasons. I'd never owned a turntable. The bat still stood in its place by the cabin door but the albums, 23 in all, had been knocked from their knee-high perch on a shelf. Danny George was taking photos when I walked in.

"Somebody was looking for something," said Natalie Heath not looking at me.

"You mean something worth stealing," I asked.

"Maybe, but it feels like they were looking for something in particular. Look at your Fiesta ware," she said. I couldn't because I didn't know what Fiesta ware was. She recognized my lost look, sighed, then pointed to the colorful plates and bowls, that had come with the boat, sitting on the countertop. "They've been removed from the cabinets and set on the counter."

My confusion settled on my face and caused my eyebrows to merge. "Okay," I said.

Exasperated, Lt. Heath said, "The dishes are opaque. To see if there was anything behind the plates, they had to be moved. But the glasses are clear," she said nodding to the next shelf. "so, they didn't need to be moved. There's not much room behind those plates, so they were looking for something small. Any idea what they were looking for?"

I tried to dodge the question. "Maybe it was a random break-in?"

"Nice move on dodging the question, you should run for office. You've got yachts on either side of you twice as big and four times as expensive. So, what were they looking for Paxton?" she asked again.

"It's a long story and I've got a call to make," I said nodding my head in the direction of Danny George, now dusting for fingerprints. "Let's go up top and sit."

I needed both hands to climb the ladder to the top-deck, so I waited until I got up there to call in the flash I'd just gotten.

He was drunk now, but when sober, was a respected surgeon. Over a long career, he had been very careful never to injure his valuable hands. No volleyball or digging in the garden for him. So, when he tripped down the steps to his pool, his reflexes were tuned to avoid injuring those precious hands. His face took the brunt of the blows on steps 5,6, and 7.

When I finished telling Heath the Threadgill saga and the tale of the possibly missing 1933 Double Eagle, she whistled. "Who knows about this?"

"Well there's everyone who's signed a confidentiality agreement with Sarah Koenig; and I'd rather you didn't mention this part; my best bud, Cliff Reilly and his gal-pal, Teresa Cooper."

Heath, who'd been taking notes on a small laptop, stopped and looked at me. "Did you just say "gal-pal?".

"Don't write that down."

She slapped the laptop shut.

"When Danny's done, have a look around and see if anything's missing. Unless we get lucky with fingerprints, I don't see that further investigation by LMPD is warranted. No one has reported a theft from Origins Bank. Unless you find something has been taken, I don't see anywhere to go with this. K of C doesn't have a security camera."

Nothing had been taken from Bloomers. I picked up my mother's record albums and my father's baseball bat. Danny George had assured me the cabin door would open just as fast with a credit card should I ever forget my key. I cleaned and straightened the cabin after Heath and George had departed. I locked the door behind me and was heading for my car when I saw Richard Bush lurking a few boats down. He approached me with a 9" x 12" manila envelope. "What's this," I said setting the albums and bat down on a picnic table.

"It's your visitor," Richard said, smiling with a row of teeth that recalled tombstones in a long-abandoned cemetery. The envelope contained two, time stamped photos of a stranger entering and leaving Bloomers.

"What the hell? How did you get these?"

"A couple of weeks ago, you said somebody had been on your boat, so I borrowed some gear from a friend. The camera is set up in the rocks there," he pointed to the embankment twenty-five feet beyond the bow, "It works on a motion detector."

The time stamp on the first photo was 6:58AM, before sunrise. It was too dark and grainy to be of use, but the second one caught the man coming out my door at 7:42AM, looking toward the rising sun. White guy, short hair and beard, tall and a total stranger. Richard didn't know him either. I took the photo and went back to my cabin door and held up the photo to get an idea of the guy's height. 6'2" or 6'3".

"Looks like they won't find his fingerprints," I said when I noticed the man in the photo wore black gloves.

"Why'd you waited until the police were gone to show me this?" I asked.

"Yeah," Richard said shyly, "I'm a little nervous around cops."

"Well look, this is great, I'll see that they get to the right people."

Richard handed me a USB stick, "Here's the originals. There are more, but the two I printed are the best."

"Thanks," I said again.

CHAPTER FIFTY-FOUR

This Vulcan persona was taking its toll on me. By now, the more violent incidents were waking me with a jolt and not only was I being awakened, so was Malika. I was getting so many flashes around the clock, I insisted, over Malika's objection, that I sleep on the living room couch. I didn't want her to become as sleep deprived as I was.

Just after midnight on Tuesday morning, I came home from my shift and tip-toed into Malika's apartment. She was asleep on the couch, her back to the door. My brain was fogged by exhaustion but I still got her message: if anybody is going to sleep on the couch it would be her. For a moment, I stood in the dim glow of a night light she'd left on for me and enjoyed the sensuous curve of her body under the thin white sheet. I was in love with this thoughtful, beautiful woman.

Louisville has a chain of mini-mart/gas stations branded with the name Gurgles. Open 24/7, the small, three store chain is a local start-up by two twenty-something single brothers who pooled their trust funds. Their vision was to pick one long, major transportation artery and eventually own all the gas stations along that heavy commuter route. Their artery of choice was Third Street which runs for almost 14 miles starting at the bank of the Ohio River.

The brothers spent a lot of time in Las Vegas hatching their plans for the stores and that's where they picked up their "best" design ideas. The Gurgles stores had lots of bright, flashing lights and neon. The staff uniform is pirate attire, including knee-high black boots and an eye patch. The black eye patches allow a 50% transparency and are a nuisance. Employees who wore glasses were exempt, so all employees wore glasses, some just frames without lenses.

A surprising money maker for the stores are the slot machines the guys put in each store. According to Kentucky state law, the only kind of gambling allowed in stores is the sale of lottery tickets, which is why the sign at eye level above each slot machine declares, "By law this machine delivers no pay out." The only thing a player can, in fact, win are free spins of the wheels. These one-armed bandits are a perfect fit for the pirate theme of the store. They were strategically placed between the cash register and exit door, so rather than dropping that change in your pocket, you are tempted to give the lever a pull. The machines don't discriminate, they accept all coins from all people. Every week, a patron will walk in with pockets bulging with coins, ask to borrow the stool kept behind the counter and begin an earnest attempt to win three cherries on the display. When that third cherry rolls to a stop, the customer is rewarded with a flashing light, a ringing bell, a digital banner crawl announcing three free games and the musical sound of their coins tinkling into the locked cabinet below the device.

If you look at Louisville from 30,000 feet and have a little imagination, you might see half a pie. The Ohio River would be that cut that was made to divide the pie in two. The curved, crusty, outer edge of the pie would be an outer ring road named to honor a politician who was able to squeeze out federal funds to build it. Now, cut that bottom half of the pie into four equal pieces and that first cut on the left would be 14 miles long and be called Third Street.

Twenty minutes after I'd gone to bed and nineteen minutes after I'd gone to sleep, I jerked awake with a flash of a beating at a Gurgles store in the 7000 block of South Third Street.

The beating happened by the tire pump of a Gurgles out by the crusty edge of the city's pie. Byron Bennett was a Gurgles regular who was in the store several times every day. Gurgles' cigarettes were the principal draw for Bennett though he got most of his groceries and, of course, the gasoline for his truck there too. Gurgles had the lowest price in town for cigarettes and Bennett bought his, one pack at a time in the belief that if he ever did decide to quit smoking, he would find it easier if he didn't have a half a carton still remaining under the seat of his car.

Nik Blinder was mad at Gurgles for firing him six months before. Blinder had no appreciation for what an achievement it was to get fired from Gurgles. The company paid the minimum wage and to become a senior member of the staff, you only had to hang on to your job for nine months. In the six months Blinder worked there, he had not called or showed up for work three times and failed two drug tests that he had been warned of in advance.

When his father had thrown him out of the house, telling him a 30-year-old should have his own place, Nik moved into the single car garage of his friendly neighborhood crack dealer. That had been okay but he had recently realized that this global warming thing he'd heard about wasn't going to get here by winter. His thin mattress tossed on a concrete floor would not do. But he had a score to settle before he could worry about all that.

Smoking crack fueled Blinder's aggressiveness and paranoia and clarified for him that all of his problems were the fault of Gurgles for firing him. He would show them. Nik "borrowed" his father's 22 caliber pistol from his night stand drawer while dear old mom and dad were at their jobs making custom t-shirts.

At Gurgles, Blinder parked his motor scooter 50-yards away in an empty church parking lot. He kept his helmet on to mask his identity. He walked to the store. Nik wore black cargo pants with big pockets, perfect for concealing the pistol, but that wasn't cool, so the gun rode uncomfortably in the waistband of his pants like any proper bad-ass would carry it. As soon as he stepped off the sidewalk onto Gurgles property he saw Bennett squatting besides his truck, butt crack prominent, putting air in a tire.

Bennett and Blinders knew each other from when Nik had worked at Gurgles. They bonded over smoking the same brand of cigarettes, the Dunhill Switch. The Switch, Blinder learned from Bennett, comes about when you squeeze the bubble of liquid mint in the filter and change the taste to menthol in mid-smoke. Now, seeing Bennett messed up the fuzzy plan Nik had to walk into Gurgles and shoot whoever was behind the counter.

Taking a quick look around, Nik pulled his pistol and clocked Bennett on the head with the barrel of the gun twice before Bennett could see his face. The first blow knocked Bennett out, the second fractured his skull. Nik Blinder thought Byron Bennett must be dead. He wasn't.

Blinder got on his motor scooter and went back to his garage home. Most of what Nik had learned in his life, he had learned from TV. And from TV, he knew that a teardrop shaped tattoo up by his eye told all, you had murdered someone. So, he got to work on his tattoo collection by doing one on himself. His most prominent tatt was of a green snake that encircled his neck several times. The snake's head was on Blinder's long, thin throat, its mouth was open with fangs and forked tongue, poised to strike. Blinder spent hours in front of a mirror moving his Adam's apple to make the snake come alive. He was so proud of his snake that he couldn't bring himself to cover it.

When he smashed Byron Bennett on the head, Nik had worn his helmet and kept his face turned from where he knew the security cameras to be, but his snake was preening under the bright, metal halide bulbs that illuminated every square foot of the Gurgles property.

If I hadn't already given 911 Nik's name, they would have learned his identity via the snake tattoo, but the process would have used up a lot of shoe leather as detectives made the rounds to tattoo parlors.

With Indian ink and a sewing needle, Nik Blinder made a teardrop off his left eye. He was awarding himself a merit badge. After sleeping a while, Nik woke up, smoked some more crack and rode his motor scooter to a second Gurgles location on Third Street. This one was about half-way along that slice of the pie, about half the distance to downtown Louisville.

From the shadows of bushes, Nik looked for customers inside the store. Not seeing any, he waited until the only customer at the gas pump drove away. From his months working at Gurgles, Blinder knew the clerk, Meghan Trevor, could throw a switch that would lock the doors in an instant, so he walked with purpose, head down, helmet on, to reach the door first. Meghan Trevor looked up as Blinder came through the door, gun drawn. He took aim at her chest, fired and hit her in the head. The bullet took off the top of her left ear, glanced off her skull and knocked her unconscious. Head wounds bleed a lot and Nik thought he'd killed her. He hadn't.

It was 4:07AM when I got the flash about Meghan Trevor. I had made three calls to 911 since Nik Blinders had struck at 12:30 and his name sounded familiar as I said it out-loud, but in my dog-tired condition, I didn't remember that I had named him a few hours before.

Upon leaving Gurgles, Nik Blinders stuffed his pockets with Baby Ruth candy bars to feed his crack-fired hunger for sweets. Then he went back to his garage to look in the mirror and decide if he should add another tear-drop to the same side of his face or if he should go for balance with one on the other side.

The pale, blue-green glow of the digits on the clock read "5:58" as I slowly rose from the bed and stumbled to the john. Then I opened the bedroom door a crack to see how Malika was doing on the couch. In place of her lovely form was a sheet of paper with a note that read, "Gone for milk, Love, M."

Two things hit me at once: I had told her last night that I would pick up some milk on the way home and had forgotten. Second: she had used the "L" word in her note. I had it in writing. Then I noticed in the upper right had corner, "5:55." Maybe the click of the door as she left was what really woke me.

I started to lay the paper on the kitchen table. Then I stopped. Something wasn't right.

Milk.

Gurgles Market.

I rushed back to the bedroom to get my phone. I dialed Malika's number and heard a muffled ring. I followed the sound till I found her phone wedged between the cushions of the couch she'd been sleeping on. Now it was time to panic. I looked around for her gun and didn't see it.

"Morning Pax," said the 911 operator, "what've ya got."

"Police dispatch hurry."

One click and, "Farago. What's up Vulcan?"

Sheri Farago was a retired air traffic controller, who was now a police controller. From directing airplane blips on a computer monitor, she now had control of on-duty police car blips on a similar screen.

"Sheri, has LMPD captured that guy that hit the Gurgles Mart stores? What's his name?"

"Nik Blinder. No, Pax, we haven't got him yet."

"Do we have any cars at the Gurgles on Third in Old Louisville?"

"I know where you're going with this Pax, and I had a car there, but we had a security alarm go off at a business nearby and that was the only available unit I had at the time. What's goin' on?"

"It's probably nothing," I said.

By now my pants were on, the first two of the buttons on my shirt were fastened and I was sliding my feet into the first foot ware I saw, Malika's, way too small, way too pink, flip-flops.

I explained to Sheri Farago as I pounded down the stairs. "Sgt. Kelly is on her way to Gurgles for some milk and doesn't have her phone. She doesn't know about Blinder either."

Farago was aware of all the flashes I'd called in to the police department. She knew I was sleep deprived. She knew I was her best customer. She didn't waste time trying to calm my fears and tell me I was over-reacting. Sheri Farago just said, "Sending a car right now."

The Old Louisville Gurgles location was a long block from Malika's apartment, and I ran as fast as those pink flip-flops would carry me. I passed a motor scooter with its nose stuck into some bushes as I made the turn into the Gurgles lot. I stopped near the open door when I saw Malika through the window in the back of the store at the dairy case. Hands on my knees to catch my breath, I smiled to myself at my foolishness.

Then I saw him. Helmet on, approaching the register, candy bars in his left hand and his right hand lifting his shirt tail and pulling a gun from his pants. It was all in slow motion. I screamed at the top of my voice, "GUN."

Blinder spun on his heels and fired rapidly. The first two shots missed me as I zigged and zagged fifteen feet away, but his third shot hit me full in the chest. As I fell to my knees, I saw blood pouring from the mouth of the snake that encircled Nik Blinder's neck. Then his head jerked twice more as Malika put two more rounds through the side of his helmet.

CHAPTER FIFTY-FIVE

When I talked to Sheri Farago about sending a police car to Gurgles, Carl Yates was in command at the EMS dispatch desk next to her and overheard enough to get the gist of the situation. He'd been enjoying a brief lull in an active morning. He looked at the computer screen that showed the location of all EMS ambulances and saw Unit 144 was idling three blocks away. Yates called 144 on the radio and told them to cruise by Gurgles.

My old partner, Paramedic Angela Barton with the rookie, Lee Erwin at the wheel, pulled into the lot just as I crumpled to the pavement. I don't remember much else but was told what followed went something like this: Malika and Angela ran to my side while Lee went for combat gauze. In the seconds it took Lee to retrieve the gauze, Angela gave him another order.

"We've got a sucking chest wound, oxygen and AED."

A sucking chest wound is called that because you can actually hear air rushing into the lung from the hole the bullet has made. Through the pain I managed to look at Malika, with tears pouring down her cheeks proclaiming how sorry she was. I passed out to the sound of police sirens coming from all points of the compass. Then my heart stopped.

An AED is an automated external defibrillator. It is a portable unit that measures the rhythm of the heart and sends an electrical shock to restore, or in my case start a rhythm. A modern version is a little like a robot that you attach to the patient's chest and flip the 'on' switch. The device monitors the patient and tells you what to do or what it's about to do and, in some models, shows you how to do a procedure on a built-in video monitor.

With my wound, Angela expected my heart to stop and fortunately, she had told Malika this before it happened. By the time my heart stopped, Lee had ripped open my shirt and placed one pad near my right shoulder and the other below my heart.

Then the rookie made a rookie mistake.

Lee had used the AED dozens of times in practice, but now before him was a real person, and a colleague to boot. Angela leaned in, whispering in my ear in that smooth café au lait voice, that everything was going to be alright. She rested one hand on my forehead and the other on my chest. Lee, watching only the AED monitor, anticipated the next instruction and hit the red button in the center of the device. However, the next instruction was to say "Clear" so everyone could back away. A shock of 350 joules of energy, started my heart and knocked Angela on her ass.

For the next year, Angela would make sure everyone called the quick, always excited Lee Erwin, The Chipmunk. "Lee," she would ask. "Are you referring to that Chipmunk?"

In the re-creation of the event, days later, we would surmise that Angela, in touching both my head and chest, had become a conduit for some of that electricity that jump started my heart. Just as when I was given electroconvulsive therapy for depression, Lee Erwin with the unwitting help of Angela had given me an ECT. I never had another flash. Vulcan was no more.

CHAPTER FIFTY-SIX

My surgery and recovery were blissfully restful and uncomplicated. I was released from University Hospital after four days. As per standard operating procedure, Malika was officially assigned to desk duty while her shooting of Nik Blinder was investigated, but she never left my side while I was in the hospital. Her boss, Chief Baker-Brown, came to my room to say hello and told Malika that under the "other duties as assigned" condition of her employment, he was ordering her to stay right where she was.

Among my many visitors were my Knights of Columbus neighbors, the Shepards. They told me Richard Bush had come with them but had only gotten as far as the parking lot. It seems that besides being nervous around cops, he also had a problem with hospitals. They said the K of C docks had closed for the winter and with Richard's help, they'd moved Bloomers back to winter moorings at the River Park Marina.

My brother Phil and his wife, Cindy came to see me too. Phil said I even made the evening news in Cincinnati. Before he left, he told me, "Seriously man, we have to quit meeting like this."

There was a gift-wrapped box the size of a briefcase on the kitchen table when Malika brought me back to her apartment. She'd bought me a turntable for playing my mother's 33 1/3 RPM record albums. The unit was a modern incarnation of old technology with built in speakers, Bluetooth and USB ports. I told her I loved it and the woman who gave it to me.

When my physical therapy and my twice daily walks got me in good enough shape to reach the Heine Brothers coffee shop a quarter mile from home, I felt like I'd won a 10K race. When I wasn't sleeping, I was hitting the books pretty hard, using recovery time to capture the Paramedic rating. I would carry my books in a messenger bag and sit in the coffee shop studying.

One warmer than average October morning, I got my coffee and I took a table outside. Looking across the courtyard, I saw Sarah Koenig, her back to the street, sitting with a tall, bearded man. I remembered the one French postcard, in a frame, that I still hadn't given Sarah a copy of and started toward her to mention it. The closer I got,the more familiar the man she was with started to look.

"Sarah Koenig. Hello," I said from behind her.

She turned and smiled, said, "Well hi, Paxton, how are you coming along?" It was a safe bet that everybody who knows me and a lot who don't, know about the Nik Blinder encounter. Malika's number two in the police information office got a little ambitious while Malika was looking out for me in the hospital and played up the story to the press to beat the band.

Sarah said, "Paxton Gahl, I'd like you to meet my fiancé, Dwayne Mitchell. Dwayne, this is Pax." When he stood up to shake hands, I had him. He would come up to about here if he stood in the doorway to the cabin on my boat.

After some perfunctory small talk, I made my excuses about cooling coffee and went back to my table. When I gauged that Dwayne wasn't looking my way, I took out my phone and pressed just one button.

Sheri Farago was staffing the police dispatcher's desk and answered, "Vulcan?"

"Hi Sheri; no Vulcan is no more, it's just Paxton."

"Just Paxton is plenty good enough. What's up?"

"I think I'm sitting here in a coffee shop looking at the guy who broke into my boat."

Sheri was fast. "I've got your GPS location and the folks downstairs have that photo. I'm sending a couple of cars your way and transferring your call to RTCC."

The "folks downstairs" were in the Real Time Crime Center. When I started work at the dispatch office, I had a whirlwind tour of the Emergency Communications Center.

At the RTCC there were a half a dozen people in the room, each with a half a dozen monitors on their desks as well as another 30 large TVs mounted cheek to jowl on one wall. The TVs showed real time street scenes all over the city. The RTCC has over 750 security cameras at their fingertips. Upstairs, Sheri Farago must have seen on her digital map a blip that indicated a security camera within range of where I was sitting at the coffee shop.

Barbara Mundt came on the phone. When I arrived to work in dispatch, I'd met Barbara, but the name had no face in my memory.

"Let's see here Paxton. I'm on a pole at the intersection down the street, let me zoom in. Ok, I see you. Where is the suspect?"

"He's about 20 feet to my left with a woman whose back is to you," I said.

"Got him. Now let me pull up the photo." I heard computer keys clicking.

"Ladies and gentlemen, we have a match," she said.

Sheri Farago had been listening in and she said, "Barbara could you send officers in units 296 and 384 a photo, they'll be there momentarily."

As the story unfolded, we learned that Sarah Koenig was guilty of a little pillow talk and not being good at picking boyfriends but 'high crimes and misdemeanors' were not her thing. Sarah had been excited to tell Malika and me the story of the missing gold after we'd signed the confidentiality agreement and she would have been just as excited to tell her boyfriend.

Dwayne wanted a look around my boat for himself. I wouldn't have known he'd been there if not for the throw rug being two inches from where it was supposed to be. Sarah told Dwayne about the clues that led to the discovery of the Krugerrands.

Dwayne must have been furious about not finding the postcards and he came back to Bloomers for a more thorough and destructive search.

The next day I looked for and found the framed postcard right where I'd left it in the stack with my mother's record albums. I paged through the stack of records. James Taylor, Joni Mitchell, Crosby, Stills and Nash, Carole King and I found the postcard sandwiched between Roberta Flack and Billy Joel. Among the many Linda Ronstadt albums, I picked mother's favorite to put on the turntable.

Different Drum was the album's title song and the one my mother loved to sing the most. I slouched back on the couch and listened to the song as I took the frame apart to remove the postcard.

In a line that mentions not being able to distinguish the forest from the trees, I looked at the card and saw the "forest" of that 150-year-old card: the picture, the stamp, the postmark, and the message were all very clear and very old. Then I saw the "trees." There, on the bottom was something that has become so common and ubiquitous that it has become invisible. There in the forest was a tree that didn't belong. It was a bar code.

Ubiquitous it may be, but there are dozens of different kinds of barcodes. To narrow the field, I had some facts and I made some assumptions: Norman Threadgill's route to president of the Origins Bank may have been a sure thing, but his father-in-law made certain he learned every job along the way. Banks churn out a lot of mail. The bank would have a mailroom and as a practical matter, a stamp machine and a barcoding printer to assure the lowest postage rate. Norman Threadgill could have printed any numbers he wanted using the barcode printer.

The barcode contained an address. I hoped.

A web search confirmed that mine looked like a postal barcode. The U.S. Post Office calls it the Intelligent Mail barcode. I downloaded the Post Office barcode scanner into my phone and scanned the barcode on the bottom of the post card.

The result was: 3826807685724989.

From my previous experience, I translated these numbers to:

North 38.268076   West 85.724989.

I pulled up Google Maps on my computer and entered the latitude and longitude. Then I did one of the hardest things of my life. Just like she had done for me, I waited for Malika to get home from work.

CHAPTER FIFTY-SEVEN

I was on Malika like white on rice when she came through the door.

"Hi honey, how was your day, let me take your jacket, have a seat."

I showed her the postcard barcode, the coordinates and then I woke the computer screen from the energy saving snooze it had been taking.

"Your turn to hit the button," I said.

With the flair of a ring master at the circus, she twirled her finger over her head and brought it down on the computer key that said, "ENTER."

We flew in from space like the space shuttle returning from a mission, passed over the east coast of the U.S., descended into the Ohio Valley and landed on a boat in slip number 26 at the River Park Place Marina. We were actually looking at Bloomers, at its moorings. It was as if we were seeing this in real time from a hovering helicopter.

Malika and I both deflated a couple of inches into our seats.

"It's got to be there," Malika said. "We're just not looking hard enough."

I was still not up to driving a car. Physical therapy had made it abundantly clear that turning a steering wheel was not yet in my bag of tricks. I rode downtown with Malika the next morning and had her drop me at River Road where the Belle of Louisville docks every night to rest its hundred-year-old bones. From there I continued my rehab by walking several miles east to the marina.

I had called Cliff the night before and given him the latest update. The plan du jour was for me to do another stem to stern search in the morning and then around noon Cliff would bring an engineer's eye to the party. I knew Cliff didn't look at objects the same way I did, so maybe he could see a hiding place I couldn't. If all that failed, we'd go to lunch.

This time, I brought to mind all those cops and robbers TV shows and movies I'd watched. I pulled out all the drawers from the chest of drawers, emptied them and flipped them over to see if anything was taped to the underside or back. I took the lid off the toilet tank and looked in and behind it. I looked in light fixtures and electrical outlets. A cactus plant stood as a forbidding sentinel to the flower pot in which it lived and I pulled on heavy work gloves and lifted the cactus by the trunk to look in the pot. I moved the coffee table and rug to go down in the hold to check the engine room. If my life depended on it, I could have lifted the lid, but it didn't, so I didn't.

When Cliff arrived, I was fast asleep in Bloomers' only double bed. I knew the pleasure of naps would be taken away when my gunshot wound had healed so I enjoyed them while I could. Cliff looked at places that had been searched once, twice or three times before. He pulled a powerful flashlight from his pocket and spent a half hour below deck. Then we gave up and went to lunch at the River Road Barbeque.

Back at Malika's, I sat at the kitchen table and tried to concentrate on studying for my last paramedic's exam to be taken in a week, just before Thanksgiving. I stayed at it until it was time for Malika to get home from work. I put the books away and thought I would greet her with some music coming from the turntable she'd bought me. I looked across the room to the bookshelf where we installed my new record player. On the shelf below stood my mother's record albums. Carly Simon, on the cover of her album, No Secrets, looked at me from across the room. Was it serendipity that made hers the first album in the queue? Did I unconsciously place her first because of the album title? Simon stands looking into the camera, long brown hair draped over a denim colored long sleeve shirt, her plum colored pants matched her wide brimmed hat. But it was the very feminine way she held her left hand that caught my eye. From across the room she appeared to be pointing down.

I never did get around to putting that 45-year-old vinyl platter on the turntable before Malika came home. And I was still laughing when she walked through the door.

The next morning, Malika and I, Cliff and Teresa meet at the marina. Malika cashed in on the hero status she'd earned by taking out Nik Blinder and went to the police scuba team to borrow a wet suit and snorkel gear. She told them she wanted to inspect the underside of my boat to see if it needed to be dry-docked over the winter for maintenance. I was still in high regard among the LMPD for my work in getting the guy who shot Officer Eickmann and the scuba folks were anxious to help. They offered to set up a "training exercise" that would encompass the inspection of the underside of Bloomers. Malika nixed the training exercise by pointing out the press was sure to get wind of it. Then she came away with everything she needed in a cardboard box.

In November, the Ohio River is cold. Nobody envied Malika. I moved Bloomers to an empty slip. Cliff, our resident engineer, had developed a plan when I called him the night before. Cliff and Teresa used Teresa's 100-foot clothes line to make a rope grid to sink to the bottom of slip number 26. Visibility wasn't great, but even if Teresa could see nothing, she could feel her way, one two-foot by two-foot square at a time. It took 30 minutes to lay out the grid and for Malika to gear up.

Five minutes after Malika went in the water, Teresa felt a tug on the mooring rope Cliff had attached to Malika's weight belt. Malika broke the surface and removed her mask. "Pull it in slowly," she instructed.

Cliff pulled up a round steel pipe, the caps were sealed with wax at each end. Malika said she found the pipe spiked vertically in the mud right in the center of the search grid: the center of the boat slip. Norman Threadgill had planted the pipe directly below his boat in ten feet of water.

As was his habit, Cliff had been thinking ahead, he brought along heavy work gloves, a small blue tarp and a propane torch. I handled the torch, Cliff and Malika donned the gloves, and Teresa filmed.

When the molten, mud-colored wax finally gave up its grip on the lid, a pair of silk, ruby red bloomers were the first thing that peeked out of the tube. Pulling out the bloomers, we discovered a gold chain was attached. Gently pulling on the chain revealed a gold coin encased in a protective plastic container. I cradled the coin in my hands and read aloud, "1933." I was holding an Augustine Saint-Gaudens, Double Eagle worth seven and a half million dollars.

CHAPTER FIFTY-EIGHT

Sarah Koenig managed to keep her job at Origins Bank. I suppose after the board of directors found the last president of their bank was a thief on a grand scale, Sarah's sins were small potatoes. It was the second week in December and Sarah had invited Malika, Teresa, Cliff and me to meet her at the bank. The first thing we saw when we all walked into the conference room was four copies of a confidentiality agreement on the table in front of four of the chairs.

Sarah offered us coffee and we sat. Ms. Koenig explained that a bank has no liability for what is in or not in a safety deposit box. The bank's insurance company also has no liability. However, the family of Isadore Kosta who had rented the box in 1987 was very grateful that all the gold had been found. Likewise, Origins Bank would be very grateful if word did not spread that a former bank president had stolen from one of its customers.

"I'll skip to the bottom line," Sarah said. With that, she walked to a side table and returned with a briefcase which she laid flat on the table. She popped the spring-loaded locks and lifted the lid. "Your finder's fee," she said, "in exchange for your signatures on those pieces of paper." We signed.

Stacked in rows like chips at a roulette table were the 270 Krugerrands from the Twelve Mile Island find. We had never expected to see these coins again.

Then the troubles began. Cliff and Teresa denied they were entitled to any of the finders' fee. M and I disagreed vehemently with them. To conduct these delicate financial negotiations, we told them discussions would re-commence over dinner, our treat.

Malika and I sat across the table from our antagonists. The venue was a fancy Italian restaurant in downtown Louisville. Malika and I couldn't have afforded to darken the doorway of this restaurant the week before, but here we were. Our strategy was to ply our quarry with wine and pasta. The carbohydrates would make them lethargic and we could bend them to our will.

The breakthrough came before dessert. Cliff and Teresa relented enough to admit they had been "some" help in finding the coins. If we insisted, a fee akin to an engineer's hourly consulting fee would be ok.

Malika and I exchanged a brief look of disappointment. We didn't have to say anything, this would not do. Desserts arrived and the subject of gold coins was dropped. Instead Teresa entertained us with the story of how a young man had called her jewelry store and explained that he needed his high school class ring cut off. Cutting a ring off of someone's finger is not uncommon in her business. Knuckles grow and rings don't, fingers get jammed and swell, etc. But the young man went on to explain the ring was stuck, "someplace it shouldn't be." Teresa would later explain to the embarrassed lad why the other stores he called had hung up at that point. They thought they were on the receiving end of an obscene phone call. Teresa was made of tougher stuff for which she credited her mother who once upon getting an X-rated phone call asked the stranger to hold on till she pulled up a chair and lit a cigarette.

It turns out the young man's pet boa constrictor had slithered through the ring as it lay on his desk and since the snake's skin had scales like a fish, it couldn't get out the same way. Her bench jeweler liberated the snake by cutting the ring off.

Maybe it was the mention of jewelry that sparked an idea of how to get Cliff and Teresa to accept a fair share of coins. Excusing myself to go to the restroom, I tapped the side of Malika's shoe and she followed me a moment later. I waited in a noisy hallway amid the traffic of wait staff bustling to and fro with clanking dishes. I was smiling in her direction as Malika rounded the corner, a busboy was not far behind. I got as far as, "I have an idea," when the load the busser was carrying shifted as he turned into the kitchen. Dishes clattered. In the midst of this din, I finished the second part of the sentence, "they'll get married," and Malika sprang into my arms kissing me before I could finish. I like being rewarded for good ideas as much as the next guy, but she hadn't even heard the best part, which was meant to be: "and we'll pay for the honeymoon, first class as a wedding gift." But I immediately realized she thought I said, "We'll get married."

For weeks, I had been trying to find the best way, not to mention the courage to ask "the question" and now it was being handed to me on an antipasto platter. I landed on my feet faster than ever in my life and added, "If you'll have me."

I was the accidental fiancé. I plucked a napkin ring off the overloaded tray of a passing busser, got down on one knee and slid it on three fingers of Malika's left hand.

The traditional engagement method wasn't going to work for Cliff either. He couldn't buy an engagement ring and pop the question because he had to buy the ring from her. He made do by proposing on Christmas Eve after the boys had gone to bed.

The practical among us (Malika and Cliff) suggested a double wedding. We had so many friends in common, it made sense and sounded like fun. Malika and Teresa planned the wedding without telling us anything about it. Cliff and I planned the honeymoon(s) in total secrecy.

The wedding ceremony, with the aid of our boating friends at Knights of Columbus, was on Twelve Mile Island. A Unitarian minister, who for no obvious reasons, was called Big Kathy, conducted the ceremony. The wedding reception was at a bowling alley near the airport. The honeymoon Cliff and I surprised our wives with was on the island of Maui. I cashed in a dozen Krugerrands to pay for the first-class trip.

The wedding was on a day in May that must have been just the kind of spring day the planners of the first Kentucky Derby had in mind when they picked that time of year for their grand horse race. There had been some early morning rain and the city glistened like a picture postcard.

The End

Acknowledgements

Thanks to every teacher I ever had, especially:
Tom Hagan
Professor Ian Stansel
Silas House

Kathy Magnuson, R.N.
Steven B. Lippmann, MD
Lt. Col. Carl Yates of the Jefferson County Sheriff's Office
Fire Chief Rick Harrison (Retired)
Eric Carlson, MD
Natalie Walters, EMT
Stephen Legge, EMT
James A. Carter, PE
Natalie Lund
Lee Moore, PharmD
Andrew Farah, MD
Stuart Monohan, Assistant Chief, St. Matthews Fire & Rescue
EMS Director Mike Riordan and the EMTs of St. Matthews Fire & Rescue
Bobbie Aubrey
Rob Schuhmann
Kathy Rogers
John Clark, Publisher
Rodger Payne

Thanks to all the brave friends who read the manuscript before the warts were
removed.

ABOUT THE AUTHOR

Before sitting down to write his first book, Joe Kremer set about to collect a wealth of life experience. He earned a degree in cartography and circled the globe as a satellite surveyor for the U.S. Department of Defense. Returning to Louisville, he convinced his high school sweetheart to marry him and became a master bench jeweler. After winning international awards for jewelry design and manufacturing, Kremer returned to his life-long passion, writing. His curiosity about shock therapy came about when his wife Kathy had that treatment and from hearing stories from a good friend who is an ER psych nurse. Joe Kremer lives in Louisville, Kentucky with Kathy and their anti-social cat Manfred.

CPSIA information can be obtained
at www.ICGtesting.com
Printed in the USA
FSHW021809011020
74276FS

9 781938 462450